Usborne
ILLUSTRATED
NORSE
MYTHS

Usborne
ILLUSTRATED
NORSE
MYTHS

Retold by
Alex Frith and Louie Stowell

Illustrated by
Matteo Pincelli

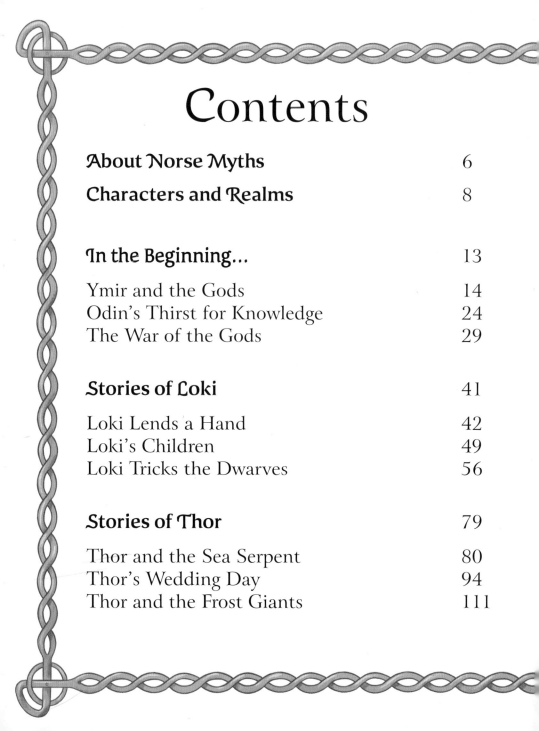

Contents

About Norse Myths

Norse Myths are the stories told by the Norsemen, often known as Vikings, who lived over a thousand years ago in lands to the far north: Denmark, Sweden, Norway and Iceland. During long winter nights they shared stories that fired their imaginations and their fighting spirit.

The myths are set in nine magical realms, bound together by a mighty ash tree, Yggdrasil. Humans lived in a place named Midgard, but within the eight other realms dwelled gods and goddesses, giants and dwarves, dragons and many other amazing, monstrous creatures.

ICELAND

NORWAY

SWEDEN

DENMARK →

BRITISH
ISLES

NORTHERN
EUROPE

Characters and Realms

ASGARD

Realm of the warrior gods, known as the Aesir. The main Aesir gods are...

Odin, king of Asgard and father of many gods, known as the Allfather. The son of Bor, he has three brothers: Vili, Ve and Honir.

Frigg, queen of Asgard. Goddess of marriage and motherhood, she is known for her kindness.

Thor, the thunder god. Son of Odin, he loves fighting, feasting and drinking.

Loki, a child of giants who lives in Asgard and has god-like status. He loves adventures, mischief and trickery.

VANAHEIM

Realm of the Vanir, the fertility gods. The main Vanir gods are...

Njord, king of Vanaheim. God of the sea, he is noble, wise and stubborn.

Frey, son of Njord and god of fertility and creativity.

Freya, daughter of Njord and goddess of love and beauty.

JOTUNHEIM

The rocky, mountainous realm of the giants.
There are two races of giants...

The frost giants, huge
creatures made entirely of
ice. Most are brutal and
violent and hate the gods.

The stone giants, who are
incredibly strong and tough.
Often short-tempered, they
are quick to fight.

NIDAVELLIR

The realm of the dwarves, who live
underground in caves and potholes...

Dwarves are short and
stubborn. Many are skilled
craftsmen, who love gold and
precious jewels.

NIFELHEIM & HELHEIM

The realms of the dead. Evil men pass through
Helheim to die again in Nifelheim, a gloomy
place of ice, snow and eternal darkness.
Helheim is ruled over by...

Hel, a gruesome queen, half young
and beautiful, half old and rotten.
Hel is the daughter of Loki.

MUSPELHEIM

A burning hot realm of fire. Anyone who does
not belong to this realm cannot endure the heat.
Muspelheim is ruled over by...

Surt, an evil demon.
He has a flaming
sword and waits for his
chance to burn down
the entire world.

There is also the realm of **Alfheim**: home to the light
elves, but this is barely mentioned in the surviving myths.

IN THE BEGINNING...

Before the world existed, there was only a place of fire, a place of ice and a great gap between them. There was no earth and no sky, no people or living creatures of any kind. But sometimes, a wind stirred up, blowing tongues of flame across the gap. The fire licked the edges of the ice, and formed the very first living thing – an evil frost giant, named Ymir...

Ymir and the Gods

Ymir was colossal. When he took his first step, his leg reached all the way across the great gap, into Muspelheim, the realm of fire. He screamed in pain as his toes began to melt, and hurled himself back into Nifelheim, realm of ice.

But it was too late. Great globs of water dripped down from his feet and fell to the ground. There, they formed into a race of smaller giants – giants of frost and giants of stone.

As Ymir began to carve new toes for himself a gush of fiery wind blew past, scorching yet more of the land of ice. Out of the thaw came another living creature – a huge cow, named

Audumla. Rivers of milk flowed from her udders, and Ymir drank from them.

In turn, Audumla licked at the salty ice of Nifelheim. And as she licked, a manlike shape began to appear – first his hair, then his head and by the third day, she had licked him free from the ice. She named him Buri. He was big and strong and beautiful.

"What kind of creature are you?" Ymir asked, peering down at him. He poked Buri with the tip of his finger, and shuddered. Buri's flesh was warm to the touch.

"You don't belong here, flesh thing!" he roared. He kicked Buri, sending him flying into the great gap.

But as Buri fell, a giantess reached out and grabbed him. "*You* will be my mate," she said.

Buri and the giantess had a son, Bor. In turn, Bor married and had three sons: Odin, Vili and Ve.

"You are the first gods," declared Bor, "and will be known as the Aesir. One day you will rule this realm and all others."

As time passed, Odin and his brothers grew to hate Ymir and his unruly, brutal gang of giants. Eventually, they attacked Ymir and killed him, before throwing his body into the great gap.

Icy blood gushed out of Ymir's wounds, drowning the race of giants. Only two escaped, in a wooden boat, riding the rivers of blood.

Odin, Vili and Ve began to make the world from Ymir's remains. His bones and his teeth became mountains and rocks, and his body became the

earth. From Ymir's blood they made inland lakes and a vast, rocking sea, which they ringed around the world.

The gods raised Ymir's skull and made the sky from it. They tossed his brains into the air to make every kind of cloud.

Then the three gods took sparks of fire from Muspelheim and flung them high in the sky to be the sun, moon and stars.

Next, the gods began to divide up the land. To the race of giants, thriving once more, the gods gave the rocky, ocean coasts, and named this realm Jotunheim. The vast inland earth was named Midgard, or Middle Earth. The gods made trees from Ymir's hair and a huge wall from his eyebrows, which they circled around Midgard, to protect it from the raging giants.

One day, when walking by the sea, the gods found two trees, an ash and an elm. From these trees, the gods created the first people. Odin breathed life into them, Vili gave them the power to think and feel, and Ve opened their eyes and mouths. They clothed them and gave them names. The ash became the first man, Ask, and the elm became the first woman, Embla. The gods gave the first people Midgard as their home, for them and their descendents.

Midgard was green and warm. There was wind, too, for sailing ships and to stir fire. The wind was created by a giant eagle. When he flapped his vast wings, the wind blew out in great gusts across the earth.

In Jotunheim, a giant had a daughter called Night, who was dark eyed and dark haired. She

also had a son, Day, who was radiant and fair. Odin took Night and Day and gave them each a chariot and two horses and set them in the sky to ride across the world. Night rode first, covering the world in darkness. Day rode behind her, his radiance lighting up the earth and sky.

Down on Midgard, a man named Mundulfari had two children, whom he thought so beautiful, he named them Sun and Moon.

"My children shine with such luminous brightness," he proclaimed, "they are surely more dazzling than the gods themselves."

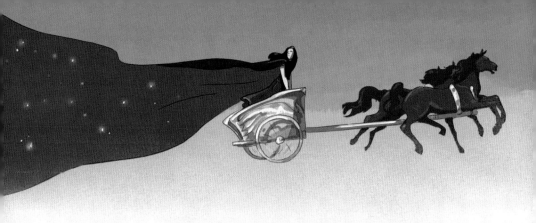

"How dare you!" roared Odin. "No human can rival the gods for beauty. As punishment, I will take your children away."

Odin whisked them up into the sky, and gave them each a chariot too. One chariot held the sun; the other the moon. Snapping and growling at their heels were two fearsome wolves, who chased the chariots in a neverending race across the skies.

After this, the gods remembered that there had been maggots crawling in Ymir's body. They turned these into dwarves – small, stocky,

human-like creatures, and sent them to live in a
realm north of Midgard, called Nidavellir. Here,
the dwarves made their homes in darkness, in
underground caverns, rocky hillsides and
dank grottoes.

Now the gods had made the first man and
woman, and set Night and Day and Sun and
Moon in the sky. They had created new realms
and filled them with men and with giants and
dwarves, and they had surrounded these lands
with sea. It was time to make their own realm.

They called it Asgard, and they made it
beautiful and strong, with shining palaces and
fertile lands, protected by towering walls. A
goddess, Frigg, was born out of the ground and
became Odin's wife. Their son, Balder, was the
noblest of all the gods.

Odin went on to father more gods, including Thor, god of thunder, Tyr, god of war, and Vidar, god of vengeance; and he took the name Allfather for himself.

From Asgard to Midgard they built a flaming rainbow bridge and named it Bifrost. They made it with skill and cunning and they made it strong.

And around all the realms of the world grew a giant tree, Yggdrasil, the world tree. It soared over everything. Its leaves dripped dew and it was forever green.

Odin's Thirst for Knowledge

Odin, Allfather of the gods, longed to learn the secrets of all the realms. He knew that Yggdrasil, the world tree, had three mighty roots. The first drank from the well of Urd in Asgard itself, and was tended by the Norns, women who controlled the destiny of all living things. Odin decided to climb down the second root, following it deep into the mountains of Jotunheim, realm of the giants.

Here, Yggdrasil's root led to a well, guarded by a gnarled, ugly god named Mimir. "Let me drink from your well," Odin called out.

"No," said Mimir. "This water isn't for me to

share. It holds the secrets of the universe itself."

"I am the Allfather," cried Odin. "I demand a drink!"

"What can you possibly give me in return?"

"My eyes have seen many wondrous things. I will give you one of them."

Mimir agreed, and watched as Odin plucked out one eye and placed it in a cup. Odin drank from the well and learned many secrets, but the water also made him thirsty for more knowledge.

He followed the third and deepest of Yggdrasil's roots. Down, down he went, seeing nothing and no one, until a squirrel scampered past him. "Little squirrel," called Odin, "what lies below?"

"Nifelheim," replied the squirrel, "the realm of ice, where the wicked go when they die." It laughed at him. "Didn't you know that? And they call you first of the Aesir, the wisest god of all!"

Odin grabbed the squirrel by its tail. "You dare to taunt me, impudent creature? Just who do you think you are?"

"I am Ratatosk. Be careful before you threaten me, one-eyed Odin! I have friends everywhere, from the Great Eagle who nests at the top of Yggdrasil, to the dragon Nidhogg who sits at the very bottom."

Reluctantly, Odin released his grip, and the squirrel raced away. Odin journeyed deeper and deeper, until a cold wind whipped around him. Odin clung tightly to the icy root.

"Go back!" shouted a voice from the depths.

Odin squinted into the wind with his remaining eye, but he could see no one. "Show yourself," he called into the darkness.

"Turn back," came the voice again. "You must return to the land of the living."

"I am Odin," shouted the god, "and I go where I please. Now show yourself!"

But the wind grew stronger and louder, roaring in Odin's ears. "This is the land of the dead, and you are not welcome here," said the voice on the wind. And a whole chorus of voices chanted, "Go back, go back, go baaaaaaack!"

Odin was too stubborn to move, but the wind was relentless. At last, he stopped fighting, and began the long climb back to Asgard. But he was not giving up. If Nifelheim was the land of the dead, then to discover its secrets he himself would have to die...

Up in the hills of Asgard, Odin stood beside Yggdrasil's wide trunk. He grabbed a spear and thrust it up through his body and into the tree.

For eight days and nights, he hung from the spear, his spirit deep in the realm of the dead. There he discovered the secrets of reading and writing runes and the workings of magic. On the ninth day, Odin came back to life.

But still he wanted to know more. He built a throne in Yggdrasil's upper branches, from where he could survey all the realms. Now he could see to the edges of the world, but he wanted to hear, too. So he sent out two ravens, who returned each evening to perch on his shoulders and whisper into his ears everything they had heard. At last, Odin truly was the Allfather, lord of gods and men.

The War of the Gods

The Aesir were not the only gods. A mysterious race, known as the Vanir, had appeared to the east of Asgard, in the lofty realm of Vanaheim. At first, the gods lived alongside each other in peace until, one day, a mischievous Vanir goddess paid a visit to Asgard.

"My name is Gullveig," she told the Aesir, and began to delight them with her magic. She conjured fire out of thin air, painting beautiful shapes with the flames and turning them into gold. Then she told the gods what they would do the next day. Each god was amazed when all her predictions came true.

Odin was fascinated. "I know the secret of runes," he boasted, "and I have learned much of the art of magic. But even with all my skill, I can't think how you perform these tricks. I demand to know the secret."

Gullveig laughed. "Why, there is no secret. These tricks are child's play to the Vanir. It comes naturally to us."

"Teach me, then," insisted Odin.

"But you are an Aesir, a warrior god," came the reply. "Your kind revels in violence. We Vanir are gods of the earth – we care for the plants and make them grow. We're so different, I couldn't teach you if I tried."

Odin shook with rage. He couldn't bear the idea of not knowing something. "Take this witch and burn her!" he shouted.

The Aesir tied Gullveig to a wooden stake, and lit a fire beneath her. Gullveig laughed, even as her body was consumed by flames. Soon, she was no more than a heap of ash on the ground.

Moments later, a wind blew up. The ash swirled in the air and took on the shape of a woman. The Aesir watched, astonished, as Gullveig's body re-formed, skin, hair, clothes and all.

"Burn her again!" roared Odin. But again, Gullveig disintegrated, only to re-form as soon as the fire burned out. She laughed maniacally.

The Aesir threw spears into Gullveig, and burned her body a third time, but she would not stay dead.

In the end, Odin worked some magic of
his own. Realizing he could not kill the Vanir
sorceress, he banished her forever, casting her
down to a damp and dreary corner of Midgard.

Njord, king of the Vanir and god of the wind
and waves, was furious. He gathered an army of
Vanir warriors, and they thundered to the great
wall of Asgard, eager for revenge.

The wall was high enough to keep out the
tallest of the giants, but it could not withstand
the Vanirs' magic. A powerful spell crumbled the
stones, and Asgard lay open to attack. The Vanir
marched with weapons raised, ready to meet the
Aesir army.

But instead, they were met by a single god,
Odin himself. "Have you to come to fight us
alone, arrogant Odin?" asked Njord. "Or are you

here to offer your surrender?"

"Why should I surrender?" snorted Odin. "My son's army has already invaded Vanaheim."

"You're lying."

"Am I? Use your magic to see for yourself."

Njord cast a spell, peered into the clouds and saw Tyr, the bravest of the Aesir, marching through Vanaheim, a great army behind him.

Beside Tyr were his two generals: Honir, Odin's youngest brother, and Balder, Odin's son. And striding through the ranks was the goddess Frigg, who had the power to heal any wound.

"Attack!" cried Tyr, and his army charged into Njord's great stone hall, killing the guards and smashing down the walls. In no time, they had reduced the hall to rubble.

Far off in Asgard, Njord felt the damage to his

home deep in his bones. He turned to his son, Frey. "Odin must pay for this insult!" he hissed. "Begin the attack on Asgard."

"I am ready, Father," replied Frey. He raised his sword-arm and, with a blood-curdling cry, he and his army began to charge.

Odin didn't move. With a gloating smile, he blasted on a trumpet and his son, Thor, came storming into battle in a chariot pulled by two ferocious goats, Toothgnasher and Toothgrinder. Their hooves pounded so hard, great peals of thunder shook the nine realms.

Thor swung a sword at Frey as he passed him, and Frey countered with a mighty clang. Frey knew he was no match for Thor in battle skills, but he didn't need to be. He had a secret weapon – a magic sword.

Frey let go of the blade and backed away.
His sword sprang to life, and flew through the
air as if controlled by an
unseen hand. Thor
jumped from his
chariot and
battled the
sword with his
own, but it
countered his
every blow.

   "Stop!" Odin
cried out. "I call
a truce. Let us not see
our sons kill each other."

   "I agree," said Njord. He nodded at Frey, who
grabbed his magic sword in one hand, offering the

other to Thor as a token of peace, and the two warriors shook hands.

"Now call off your army," Njord said to Odin. "They've already destroyed my home."

"It is done," Odin declared, pointing into the distance. "Look, I have sent my ravens to tell Tyr to return to Asgard."

"And we will return to Vanaheim," said Njord.

"Or..." Odin began, "as a sign of our new-found peace, why don't you stay here in Asgard, and sit on the Aesir council."

"I like the idea of being able to keep an eye on you," Njord mused. "I agree, on one condition – you let us keep an Aesir god in Vanaheim."

"Gladly," said Odin. "Take my brother, Honir."

"Honir?" asked Njord, "What good is that simpleton?"

"My brother is no simpleton!" Odin fumed. "Why, there's no one better at considering advice. He'll make an excellent chairman for your council. But to help him, I'll send Mimir to Vanaheim too. Mimir guards the well of truth – there's little he doesn't know."

"So be it," declared Njord, and the two kings shook hands.

Njord built a new hall in Asgard, as did his son Frey and daughter Freya. The Aesir welcomed and accepted them.

But in Vanaheim, the Vanir were soon cursing Odin's name. Honir refused to help the council make any decisions unless Mimir told him what to say. And Mimir was so angry at being sent to Vanaheim, he never spoke a word.

The Vanir sliced off Mimir's head and sent it

to Odin, threatening to start a new war, but Odin did not take the bait. Instead, he covered the head with herbs so it would not rot and sang charms over it, to give it the power of speech, revealing to him all Mimir's secrets.

When Njord saw Mimir's head beside Odin's throne, he knew Odin had a great advantage over the Vanir. If war ever broke out again, he was sure the Aesir would win. He vowed to stay loyal to Odin from that day on, and always to keep the peace.

STORIES
OF LOKI

Among the gods in Asgard lived Loki. Though god-like in appearance, he was descended from giants, so it's hard to say if he was a god himself. In fact, it's hard to say anything for sure about handsome, troublesome Loki. He could change his shape as easily as snapping his fingers, and was as slippery and cunning as the child of a fox and an eel. Still, in spite – or maybe *because* – of all his tricks, Odin loved him like a brother.

Loki Lends a Hand

O ne day, not long after the war with the Vanir, a stranger in a scruffy cloak came riding over the rainbow bridge to Asgard. Loki sat watching him approach. *A mysterious stranger,* he thought. *There's no better type of visitor. I wonder what mischief he'll bring?*

"Who goes there?" called a voice. It was Heimdall, the mighty guardian of Asgard. He moved to block the stranger's path with his vast sword, muscles tensed for a fight.

"I have an offer for Odin," the stranger replied.

Heimdall patted the man down for weapons, then let him pass. All the gods gathered to hear what the stranger had to say.

"I'm a builder," he said. "I can rebuild your wall destroyed in the Vanir war. But it will take eighteen months. And it won't be cheap."

"Name your price," boomed Odin. They really *did* need a wall to keep the evil frost giants out.

"I want the sun and the moon," said the man.

The gods all started shouting angrily. "We'll have to scrabble around in the dark!" one cried.

But the builder wasn't finished. "I also want the beautiful goddess Freya's hand in marriage."

At that, the gods fell silent. A dirty, sweaty builder marry their beloved Freya? It was unthinkable. Freya herself almost fainted in horror.

"How DARE you?" roared Odin. "Get out!"

But Loki, who'd been standing quietly beside Odin until now, said, "Don't be hasty, Allfather. I have an idea." He leaned closer. "I say accept his offer," Loki whispered. "But only give him six months. He can't possibly finish that quickly, so we'll get it half built, at least, and for free."

"Oh you are cunning, Loki," Odin smiled. Then, in a voice like thunder, he said, "I accept your offer, builder, but you must complete the work in six months, not eighteen."

"Then please let me use my horse," said the builder. "I can't carry the rocks by myself."

"I don't see why not," said Odin. "Go ahead."

So the builder and his horse set to work. As the months went by, the wall went up, higher and higher. Soon, it started to look as though he'd finish the job in time. Panic spread through Asgard, and Odin was furious.

"Loki!" he bellowed. "This is all your fault. Your ridiculous scheme is going to lose us Freya, not to mention the sun and moon! You'd better stop this builder from keeping his side of the bargain, or I'll tear you into ten million pieces."

Loki cowered. "I swear, Odin, I'll stop him."

"You had better. Or... ten million pieces!"

The next day, as the builder was starting work, a beautiful glossy mare appeared from the woods. She shook her tail at the builder's horse, and the horse whinnied and ran after her.

The builder chased his horse all day and all night, but he couldn't catch it. The deadline came and went, and the wall was not finished.

The builder howled with rage. "You tricked

me, you gods," he cried. Throwing off his cloak, he stretched up and out and up some more, revealing his true form: a towering stone giant.

Before the giant could attack, Thor stepped forward. He grabbed a boulder and hurled it at the giant's head. Lightning cracked the sky, fired by Thor's fury and, with a resounding crunch, the boulder smashed into the giant's skull.

The giant crashed to the ground. There was a pause. "Well, we certainly don't have to pay him now," said Odin.

A few days later, Loki reappeared, leading an eight-legged horse. He looked at Odin with wide, sorry eyes. "This is for you," he said, handing over the bridle. "This wonderful creature," Loki added, stroking the horse's nose, "is the child of the giant's horse. It was born today, fully grown."

"And I believe I'm looking at its shape-shifting mother?" chuckled Odin. He peered at Loki more closely. Indeed, Loki still looked

a little horselike in the face, and stamped his feet just like the mysterious mare.

Loki grinned. "Guilty," he said.

Odin was delighted with his new steed, and with Loki's shape-shifting trick. So, even though the other gods grumbled, Odin forgave him.

With a huge sigh of relief, Loki swore, "I'll never get us into trouble like that again."

Odin failed to notice that Loki had slipped his hand behind his back, fingers crossed.

Loki's Children

Loki was not the only troublemaker in his family. Before Loki's children were born, the far-sighted Norns gave the gods a terrible warning: "The trickster's spawn will be the death of you."

Three of Loki's children did indeed look deadly. One was a wolf named Fenrir, another was Jormungand, a gigantic sea serpent, and a third was a demonic creature known as Hel. Half her body was young and girlish; the other half was old and rotten, like a corpse.

Jormungand and Hel were so terrifying, they were cast out of Asgard at once. "Good riddance!" Odin shouted after them.

Jormungand fell
with a tremendous splash
into the ocean surrounding Midgard,
while Hel plunged into Helheim, the
land of the dead, and became its ruler.

Only Fenrir was allowed to stay in Asgard. He
was just an ordinary wolf at first, so the gods felt
sure they could handle him. But he soon grew
into a gigantic, drooling beast, with teeth and
claws as sharp as knives.

"We will have to chain him up before he eats

someone," said Odin. He looked around. "Any volunteers?"

The gods remained unusually silent. "Loki," said Odin. "He's your child, perhaps you..."

Loki cut him off mid-sentence, with a reproachful look. "How can you ask me to tie up my own son? Please, don't make me!"

Odin held up his hands, "Fair point, Loki. Anyone else?"

But none of the other gods wanted to go near the wolf. Eventually Tyr, the god of war, stepped forward. "I will do it," he said.

The next day, he sidled up to Fenrir, carrying a huge and heavy chain. "You're such a mangy, puny beast," he taunted. "If I tie you up with this, you'll never get free."

"I could do it in my sleep," scoffed Fenrir.

The wolf let Tyr chain him, yawned, then burst the chains with a twitch of his rippling muscles.

I'll have to try a thicker chain, thought Tyr. After searching high and low, the war god found a chain that was twice as thick as the first, with links as big as dinner plates. "You won't escape from this one," Tyr promised.

Fenrir shrugged his hairy shoulders, and let Tyr chain him up once more. As the god of war wrapped the chain around and around the wolf, all the gods gathered to watch. Surely he couldn't break out of a chain as thick as this?

When Fenrir was trussed up tightly, Tyr stepped back and waited. Stiffly, Fenrir lay down, putting his head on his chained-up paws and looking very sorry for himself.

The gods sighed with relief... until the wolf

twitched his nose, flicked his tail, and tore through the chains as though they were paper.

So Tyr had to start all over again. This time, he sent a message to Nidavellir, the dark home of the dwarves. "It's time to call on the experts," he told Odin. "No one in all the realms can forge stronger steel than the dwarves."

But the dwarves didn't send back a metal chain. Instead, they had wrought a rope, smooth as silk and as slender as a finger. It hardly looked strong enough to hold an ordinary wolf, let alone a monster of Fenrir's size and strength.

Still, Tyr trusted in the amazing skills of the dwarves. "Come here!" he called to the wolf. "Compared to the last couple of chains, this little piece of string is nothing! But," he added, "if you can't burst it, I promise to let you out."

Fenrir padded forward, sniffing the rope suspiciously.

"It smells of dwarves," he growled. Along with the scent of iron and deep, dark caves, Fenrir also smelled a trap. "Very well. But when you tie me up, one of the gods must put his hand in my mouth." He curled his lip into a snarling grin. "If I can't get out, and you don't free me, someone is going to lose a hand."

Once again, Tyr was the only god brave enough to volunteer. He put his hand into Fenrir's mouth, being careful not to cut himself on the creature's lethal teeth. The other gods tied the wolf's feet with the silken rope, hoping that the dwarves really were as good as Tyr believed.

When the last knots were tied, the wolf flexed his muscles. Nothing happened. He began to struggle. The ropes only grew tighter. When he saw that it was hopeless, he let out a growl from between his teeth, "Let me out!"

But Odin refused. "You're much too dangerous to wander around freely."

Furious, Fenrir bit down hard, slicing clean through Tyr's wrist. Tyr let out a howl of agony that echoed all through Asgard.

Thanks to Tyr's sacrifice, the gods didn't have to worry about Fenrir, at least for a while. But thanks to Fenrir, Tyr spent the rest of his days with a stump instead of his right hand.

Loki Tricks the Dwarves

Early one morning, the gods were woken by the sound of wailing. Sif, goddess of the harvest, was sobbing in great gasps. Soon, her husband, Thor, was howling with rage. The rest of the Aesir quickly gathered outside Thor's hall. Frigg, queen of Asgard, hammered on the door. "What's the matter?" she called.

Thor kicked the door open and strode outside with Sif wrapped in his massive arms, her head cradled to his chest. No one could see Sif's face, or her long, bright blonde hair.

"Look what that villain, Loki, has done," shouted Thor. He drew back his arms to reveal

Sif's head. It was completely bald. Sif started
sobbing again, and Frigg came over to comfort
her, while the other gods turned to Loki.

"What makes you think it was me?" he
whined. "Anyone could have done it. Where's
your proof?"

"I don't need proof," roared Thor.
"It's in your nature to cause
mischief, so it must
have been you." He
grabbed Loki and
hoisted him up.

Odin quickly
stepped forward. "It's
true that Loki likes to play
tricks, Thor, but that doesn't
mean he's the cause of *all* mischief."

Thor snarled and let Loki fall to the ground. He was turning away, when something caught his eye. "Ha! What's this on your shoulder, lying Loki? It's a strand of Sif's hair – the gold is unmistakable!"

Loki opened his mouth to protest, but for once he could think of nothing clever to say. "Very well, Thor, I confess. It *was* me," he said with a shrug. "I crept into your bedroom last night and cut off Sif's hair. But it was worth it to see the look on your face!"

Thor raised his fist, ready to bring down a thundering blow on Loki's head.

Odin grabbed Thor's arm, and pulled him away. "I know you're angry, Thor, but let's find another way to settle this. Loki, you can put that cunning brain of yours to good use for once. To make it up to Sif, you must turn her hair into *real* gold, and return it to her head. I will be watching – see that you account for every last strand!"

The other gods laughed as Loki stormed off. He was beginning to regret this trick. To start with, he'd have to go all the way down into darkest Nidavellir, to visit the dwarves. Loki hated dwarves, but they were magnificent goldsmiths. Only a dwarf could spin hair into pure gold.

With Sif's hair tied up in a bundle, Loki set off. He wandered through dark and twisting tunnels, until he reached the realm of Nidavellir.

Squinting in the gloom, he found two elderly dwarves, looking at him with interest.

"My humblest greetings," Loki said, his voice dripping with charm. "Tell me – who are the finest craftsmen in Nidavellir?"

"That's easy," said one. "Every dwarf knows the sons of Ivaldi are the best."

"You're just saying that because you *are* Ivaldi!" laughed the other. "My sons, Eitri and Brokk, are far better smiths than yours."

Loki smiled. "Tell me, where can I find your talented sons?" he asked.

Ivaldi pointed to a cave behind them. "Down there."

"And my sons have a forge there," said the other dwarf, pointing to a cave opposite. Loki peered into both caves, then strode purposely to find the sons of Ivaldi.

They scowled when they saw him. "Go away, mischief-maker. We won't do any work for the likes of you."

"I come here as an envoy of Odin himself," said Loki. "Don't you dare ignore me."

"Prove it," said Ivaldi's eldest son, Dvalin.

"How else could I have obtained this?" asked Loki, and he showed them Sif's hair. It shone so brightly, the dwarves knew it could only belong to a goddess.

"Odin has sent me to find you personally," lied Loki. "He told me only the sons of Ivaldi can remake Sif's hair from gold, and make it so that it grows again."

"Odin asked for us by name?" said Dvalin, his chest puffing up with pride. "Then of course we shall help. And to show our worth, we'll make Odin a gift, as well."

"How very kind," said Loki. "But..."

"Yes?"

"It might be unwise to make a special gift *only* for Odin. The Aesir are a jealous bunch, especially that hothead, Thor."

"You're right," said Dvalin. "If we make a gift for Odin, an Aesir god, we'd better make another for the Vanir god, Frey."

Loki hissed in annoyance. He'd meant the dwarves to make a second gift for *Thor*. He was sure it was the only way Thor would forgive him.

Dvalin took Sif's hair and dipped it into a pool of liquid gold. He swirled it through the molten metal, carefully encasing each and every strand.

Then he combed the hair through with diamond dust until it sparkled like the stars.

Beside him, Dvalin's brother Berling forged a spear of the finest steel, a gift for Odin. "This spear," said Berling, "will always hit its target."

Impressed, Loki weighed the weapon in his hands. "Not bad," he murmured.

"And here is a gift for Frey," said a third son, Grer. It was a beautiful ship, small enough to fit into Loki's pocket. "When you give it to Frey, its true worth will be revealed."

Loki thanked the sons of Ivaldi, and headed to the cave of Eitri and Brokk. Holding up his gifts, Loki started to praise them loudly.

"Why, surely these are the finest creations in all of Nidavellir. I was right to seek out the sons of Ivaldi. No other team could have crafted such works of beauty fit for gods."

"Nonsense!" retorted a gruff voice. "My brother, Eitri, is the finest metalworker in all Nidavellir. He can make three gifts for the gods, each greater than those paltry offerings. I, Brokk, would bet my life on it."

"Excellent!" said Loki, "I love a good bet. I, too, will stake my own life."

"*Your life*, Loki?" asked Brokk. "Let me check. If I win the bet, I get to cut off your head?"

"Yes," said Loki. "But for a real test of skill, you must make a weapon that will make mighty Thor, god of thunder, proud to wield it." And with that, thought Loki, he was saved from Thor's wrath.

In no time at all, the brothers had made their first gift: a massive boar, with jet black skin and golden bristles. "The toughest combat beast ever born or made," explained Brokk. "It will serve its master, Frey, in battle."

Brokk and Eitri went straight to work on their next gift: a bracelet for Odin. Loki rubbed his neck worriedly. *I need a gift for Thor, but if this pair make their gifts too well, I could lose my head. It's time to take action*, he decided. *I'll have to cheat!* Seeing the dwarves intent on their task, he swiftly turned himself into a fly.

Eitri was working at the furnace, which was blasting out waves of blistering heat. Not daring to fly too close, Loki began buzzing around Brokk, who was pumping a mighty pair of bellows to keep the furnace burning. Try as he might, Loki could not break Brokk's concentration.

Loki switched back to his usual form. His eyes widened in disbelief as he saw Eitri use gallons of gold to create just one small bracelet. *Eitri must be using magic to hold so much metal in such a tiny object,* Loki thought. *But why?*

At last, Eitri held up the gleaming trinket and gave it to Loki. It was small, but incredibly heavy. "You must give this bracelet to Odin," the dwarf said. "And now, we will forge our final gift – a hammer for Thor. Brokk, get back to the bellows, and make sure you do not stop pumping, even for a moment!"

Loki took on a new form this time – a gadfly. He stung Brokk's hand, but the dwarf merely grunted, and kept working the bellows. He stung Brokk's nose, and the dwarf howled out loud – but still he did not stop pumping.

By now, Eitri had finished casting the hammer's tough steel head, and was working on the shaft. Loki could hear him chanting a complex incantation.

Desperate to keep his head, even if it meant a beating from Thor, Loki flew into Brokk's face and stung him on the eye. The pain was too great for the dwarf, and he let go of the bellows to swat the gadfly out of the cave.

"What are you doing, brother?" shouted Eitri. "The furnace must stay at its hottest! You have ruined my creation. Look – the shaft is too short."

Brokk hung his head in shame. Loki returned to his godly form, and came back into the cave.

"Well now," he said confidently, "I see you have finished Thor's hammer. But it's tiny! Do you think he's a child?"

"I know you, Loki," said Eitri, "and I know my brother. He would not have dropped the bellows unless provoked. Somehow, you cheated."

"I, a cheat?" said Loki, trying to look innocent.

"Yes!"

"Never mind that," said Brokk. "I still think our work is better than that of those no-good sons of Ivaldi! Let's go with Loki up to Asgard, and present these gifts ourselves. That way, we can claim our prize immediately."

"So be it," said Loki. And he strode as fast as he could back to Asgard, the two dwarves running after him.

When Odin heard what Loki had been up to, he called all the gods to Gladsheim, the hall of judgement.

"Fellow gods!" declared Odin. "I want you to vote on which of these gifts is the greatest."

First, Loki presented Sif with the golden hair. She placed it carefully on her scalp. Strands at the base wove themselves onto her head. She shook it and great tresses of gold fell around her shoulders, shining in the light. The gods gaped in wonder.

Loki pulled the next gift from his pocket – the wooden ship for Frey. Nonplussed, Frey took it,

but as he breathed over it, the sails billowed and grew. A great creaking resounded around the hall, and the boards of the ship began to unfold, until it filled the whole hall.

In wonder, Frey tugged a cord on one of the sails, and the ship shrank back into the palm of his hand. "It's a magnificent gift," he exclaimed.

"And this fine spear is called Gungnir," said Loki, presenting the sons of Ivaldi's final gift to Odin. He pointed it at the far end of the hall. "Try hurling it at that dark knot of wood on the door."

"I may be Allfather of the Aesir," said Odin, "but no one could hit such a target from here."

"Try, Allfather," urged Loki.

Odin drew back the spear, and the gods watched as it flew over their heads and across the hall. When it hit the dark knot, everyone cheered.

Odin smiled. "This is the finest weapon I've ever seen."

"The greatest gift so far," agreed the gods.

"Now," said Odin, turning to Brokk and Eitri, "let's see what you have to offer."

"My lord," said Eitri, "take this bracelet, Draupnir. Feel its weight. Does it not seem heavier than it ought?"

"Why, yes, it does," said Odin. "It cannot be made with pure gold."

"It most certainly *is* pure gold," Eitri replied indignantly. "The reason for its great weight is that every ninth night, the bracelet will drip eight times, and each drop will form a new bracelet, exactly the same as the first."

The assembled gods were astonished. Surely this was the finest piece of gold ever crafted, finer even than Sif's gleaming hair.

Next, Brokk brought forward the boar, which grunted loudly. "My lord Frey, mightiest of the Vanir, please accept this gift."

"What is the creature's name?" asked Frey.

"He is Gullinbursti, or shining mane. His bristles are made of the finest dwarf gold. They will light the way through the blackest of nights."

"And his hide is so tough," added Eitri, "that no weapon will pierce it. In battle, he will be formidable indeed."

Loki rubbed his neck worriedly. It was looking as if Brokk and Eitri might yet win the bet. But their hammer couldn't be a better weapon than Odin's spear, he reassured himself, as he ushered Brokk over to Thor.

"Great god," said Brokk. "Please accept this

battle hammer, Mjollnir."

Thor took it and wrapped one of his meaty fists around the handle. He held it up and stared at its great metal head in awe, imagining all the damage it could do. It was love at first sight. But his fellow Aesir were less impressed.

"Look at that stubby handle," laughed Tyr. "It's barely as big as your hand. You won't be able to throw it very far."

Thor hated to be laughed at. He snarled at the dwarves, ready to test his hammer out on them.

"Wait!" cowered Eitri. "I know the handle is short, but let me tell you Mjollnir's secret."

"What is it?" growled the thunder god.

"Whenever you throw it, no matter how near or far, it will always fly back to your hand, ready to be used again."

Thor immediately hurled the hammer at Loki, who was standing on the far side of the hall. He ducked and the hammer missed him. But, as Loki stood up again, the hammer whacked him on the back of his head as it flew into Thor's outstretched hand.

"Fantastic!" cried Thor, and he kissed Mjollnir in sheer delight.

The gods cast their votes, and even Odin agreed that Mjollnir was the finest gift. "After all," he said, "I'll need to retrieve my spear after each throw, but Mjollnir can strike again and again."

All eyes turned to Loki, who sat on the floor nursing the bump on his head.

Brokk grinned. "Now, trickster, I shall take my winnings." And he pulled a sword from his belt.

Loki gulped, backing away from the smiling dwarf. "It is true that you have won the bet," he said, "but before you strike me with your sword, consider this. I agreed you could have my head... but I never said you could take my neck." He stood up, and put his hand under his chin. "Where will you cut? Can you see a place that will remove all of my head, but none of my neck?"

Spitting with anger, Brokk admitted that he could not see where to make such a cut. "Curse you, Loki! I knew you would find a way to twist my words. Well, let's see you talk your way out of this!"

He took a needle and threaded it with a bristle from his long, bushy beard. Pinning Loki to the ground, he began to sew his lips together, until his mouth was completely sealed.

Loki jumped up and down, fuming, unable to utter a word. He ran away, and set to the painful task of unstitching his mouth. The gods roared with laughter. It was a rare day indeed when silver-tongued Loki was silenced.

STORIES
OF THOR

Thor, god of thunder, never backed down from a fight – whether against the most terrifying monster or the surliest of giants.

His enemies feared the power of his magical hammer, Mjollnir, but even without it, Thor was a force to be reckoned with.

Thor and the Sea Serpent

A grand feast was fast approaching, and Odin had a task for his son Thor. "Go to the shining sea of Asgard," he ordered, "and seek out the god Aegir. He is the only one who can brew enough mead for us all."

Thor rubbed his hands with glee. He loved mead, a delicious drink made with honey. But when he found Aegir, the god laughed at him.

"It's true I mix the best mead in the Nine Realms," he bragged, "but to make enough for everyone, I'll need a pot bigger then you!"

"Where am I going to find a pot that size?" grumbled Thor.

"That's not my problem, is it?" snorted the god. "Now go away and don't come back until you find one."

Thor scowled at Aegir and trudged back to Valhalla, where the other gods were preparing the feast. *I'm going to need help,* he thought.

He marched into the hall, waving his arms to attract attention. "Who will join me on a great and worthy quest?" he boomed.

"What quest, Thor?" asked Frey, excited. "Is there a dragon to slay, or a maiden to rescue?"

"Not as such..."

"Perhaps the frost giants are ready for a new war?" asked Tyr, eagerly.

"Not *exactly*," said Thor, sheepishly. "I need to find a pot."

"A pot?" Tyr and Frey laughed together. "What kind of a quest is that?"

"Well, it's not just any pot. It has to be a pot big enough to hold mead for all the Aesir."

"I know where to find a pot that vast," boasted Tyr. "My step-father, Hymir the giant, has one."

"Then let's pay him a visit," said Thor.

"There's just one problem..." Tyr replied. "Hymir hates gods. He only tolerates *me* because he married my mother."

"I'll fight him for the pot," growled Thor.

Tyr laughed. "You're going to fight a giant who is twice your size, and whose body was hewn from granite? This is starting to sound like a real quest at last."

The two gods made their way to Hymir's hall, which stood on the edge of Jotunheim, on the shore of the wide, raging ocean. Tyr's mother opened the door and smiled in delight.

"Tyr! Come in, you're just in time for supper," she cried, hugging her son.

"Good, I'm starving," said Thor, barging in.

"Don't be too greedy, Thor," whispered Tyr. "Remember we're here to ask Hymir for help. We don't want to annoy him."

As they entered the house, the gods saw Hymir sitting at a table, chewing on an enormous ox leg. Thor and Tyr bowed their heads in respect, but Hymir ignored them. Thor shrugged, sat down and began to eat. Tyr joined him, looking nervous.

In minutes, Thor had polished off
two whole oxen. Hymir stared for a
moment in disbelief, before
slamming his ox bone down
onto the table and lumbering
to his feet.

"How dare you come into my
house and gobble my best meat," he bellowed.
"You gods are all the same, thinking you're better
than everybody else, lording it over us."

"What of it?" jeered Thor.

"I'll show you what of it!" roared Hymir,
shaking a fist in Thor's face. "Let's settle this
right now."

Before Hymir could throw a punch, his
wife broke in. "I have a better idea. Tomorrow
morning, let's see which of you can catch the

biggest fish. That way, *you'll* have a contest, and *we'll* have food for supper."

Hymir grunted in agreement, and Tyr breathed a sigh of relief. Better for Thor to lose a fishing contest than be killed in a fight.

The next day, Hymir dragged Thor out of his bed before dawn. "Why are you getting me up so early?" moaned Thor, with a yawn.

"You've never been fishing before, have you?" said Hymir. "The best catches are made first thing in the morning. Here's another tip. You'll need some bait on your line."

If I'm going to catch a really big fish, I'll need a gigantic bait, thought Thor, grabbing an ox head from the kitchen.

The giant and the god climbed into a fishing boat, and Hymir began rowing out to sea. He rowed until they could no longer see the shore, and then rowed a little further. Thor watched as Hymir cast his net, effortlessly bringing up two huge whales with a flick of his mighty wrist.

"Let's see you catch something bigger than these!" Hymir mocked.

"Impressive," said Thor, "but for a truly great catch, we'll need to row out further still." He took up the oars and began rowing hard. Hymir was so busy tying up his whales, he didn't notice how far out they were – until the boat began to lurch and roll.

"Stop!" Hymir shouted. "You've gone too far! It'll take hours to get home from here."

"Stop fussing," said Thor, "and let me put out my bait." He hooked the ox head onto a fishing line, and threw it in the sea.

Seconds later, Thor felt a tug on the line. He heaved and heaved, but he couldn't bring in the catch. Hymir watched as Thor grunted and groaned, flexing his muscles so that his arms seemed to double in size.

Thor braced his feet on the edge of the boat, straining with all his might. At last, the line came up, pulling with it the head of a terrifying monster. Its eyes were yellow and it had fangs like spears. It opened its mouth wide and spat great gobbets of blood.

Hymir screamed in fear. "Let go! Now! That's Jormungand, the biggest serpent in the world. Put him back, you fool. His body wraps around the entire ocean. He'll kill us both!"

"I'll never let go," yelled Thor, "This is my catch and I *will* bring it home!"

But Jormungand had other ideas. It thrashed its gigantic neck, churning up huge waves, forcing Hymir to cling grimly to the side of the boat.

Thor snarled in defiance. Realizing he couldn't lift the serpent out of the water, he reached back with one hand and grabbed his hammer, Mjollnir. With a great cry, he brought it crashing onto Jormungand's head.

The blow stunned the serpent. Its head slumped down at Thor's feet. It was so heavy, the deck tipped, flooding the boat with water. Terrified, Hymir cut Thor's line, and Jormungand slipped back into the ocean.

"Are you insane, Thor?" Hymir demanded. "You nearly killed us both! The boat's full of water and we're miles from land."

"What's the matter, puny giant?" laughed

Thor. "Are you scared? Don't worry, I'll save you!" And he dived into the sea.

Thor began to swim, pushing the boat in front of him, unfazed by the weight of the stone giant and the two whales. Hymir gaped at the sight of the god powering through the waves.

As soon as they stepped into Hymir's house, Tyr rushed up to greet them, his mother close behind. "Who won?" Tyr asked.

Hymir swatted Tyr to the ground. "Thor didn't catch anything!" he spat. "You can both get out of here, and never darken my doors again!"

"Gladly," said Thor, "but first, I want your mead pot."

"What?" growled Hymir. "Why should I give you anything?"

"If you won't give it to me, I'll just take it!"

Thor roared back.

Hymir had seen what Thor had done to Jormungand. There was no way he was going to fight him. Then he had another idea. "You think you're stronger than everyone else, don't you?"

"It's true! I've never met anyone stronger than me," said Thor, puffing out his chest.

"Well, here's a challenge for you. Break this cup, and I'll give you my pot." Hymir handed Thor a glass goblet, no bigger than his fist.

"Too easy," laughed Thor, hurling it to the ground.

The cup didn't break.

"Try the door," suggested Tyr. Thor whirled around and threw the cup with all his strength. It cannoned into the door, smashing it from its hinges. The cup wasn't even marked.

It was Hymir's turn to laugh. He watched Thor bounce the cup off the walls, hurl it at the ceiling, even sit on it, his face red with frustration. Plates and bowls came tumbling off the shelves, the ground shook, the walls began to crumble.

I must stop this, thought Hymir's wife, seeing her home collapse around her. She whispered in Thor's ear. "The cup is enchanted. To break it, you need to throw it at something harder than itself. Try my husband's head!"

Thor didn't waste any more time. He grabbed the goblet from the ground and dashed it against Hymir's stone forehead. The glass shattered around the giant's face.

"Now," demanded Thor, "give me the pot!"

"Take it and go," said Hymir. "Be warned, though – if you ever come here again, I'll use my head to pulverize your precious hammer into a thousand pieces!"

But Thor had already hoisted the mead pot onto his back and was heading for Valhalla, the great feasting hall of Asgard, with Tyr running behind him.

"Well done, Thor," said Tyr, clapping him on the back. "You've survived an encounter with Jormungand, and defeated a mighty stone giant. We may have set out only looking for a pot, but it turned out to be quite an adventure after all!"

Thor's Wedding Day

Thor and his hammer, Mjollnir, were never parted. He loved it so much, he even slept with it under his pillow. But, one terrible morning, he woke to find it missing.

It has to be Loki playing tricks, thought Thor. *It's always Loki*. Thor was so angry he could barely speak. Instead he flung open the shutters on his windows and let out a blood-curdling cry. "Aaaarghh! LOKIIIII! I'll kill yooooouuuuuuu!"

Dressed only in his nightshirt, Thor rushed to Loki's home, and dragged him outside. "Where... is... my... hammer?" he shouted, spitting with rage, his hands wrapped around Loki's neck.

Loki coughed, spluttered and desperately waved his finger at his mouth, trying to make Thor understand that he couldn't speak while being throttled. Thor finally let Loki drop to the ground.

"It – hhhhh – wasn't – hhhhh – me," rasped Loki, between long, gasping breaths. "I'm not insane, Thor! I wouldn't dare lay my hands on Mjollnir, much less steal it."

"If not you, then who?" demanded Thor. "You're the cause of all trouble around here!"

"I don't know," said Loki, "but I'll help you find out. Come with me." And he strode off to Freya's hall. Baffled, Thor followed

"What are we doing here?" he asked. "Surely you don't think Freya took my hammer? She's so beautiful, men are always giving her gifts. She'd never need to steal anything."

"It's one of those gifts I need. Now, be quiet and let me do the talking," Loki ordered, knocking on the door.

"What can I do for you, mischief-maker?" asked Freya, opening the door with a frown. "I heard Thor screaming your name so I know you've been up to no good again."

"I haven't," Loki insisted. "In fact, I've come here on Thor's behalf, to ask for your help."

"It's true," said Thor, pushing Loki aside. "Loki may be a lying weasel, but he's the best chance I have of finding my hammer. It's been stolen."

"What?" cried Freya. "Someone dared to steal Mjollnir? We must get it

back. How can I help?"

"Lend me your feathered falcon cloak," said Loki. "I'll use it to fly to Jotunheim. I don't know exactly who took Thor's hammer, but I'm willing to bet it was one of those evil-hearted frost giants."

"Curse them all!" wailed Thor. "I'll bring down such a storm on their heads they'll wish they'd never been born! I'll fry their brains with my lightning bolts, I'll pound them flat, I'll..."

"Be patient, Thor," Loki interrupted. "Let me find out which villain has done this, and then you shall have your revenge."

As he wrapped Freya's falcon cloak around his body, his arms became wings. Flapping them in delight, Loki soared into the sky.

He flew up to the highest peaks of Jotunheim,

but saw no sign of the hammer. He swooped through narrow gorges and over rocky caverns, into the very heart of Jotunheim, where frozen rivers wound their way around snow-capped mountains.

With eyes as sharp as a falcon's, Loki at last made out the unmistakable shape of Mjollnir's wide head and short handle, lying on the edge of a gleaming lake of ice. "What's it doing there?" Loki wondered.

He glided down to the lake and shrugged off the cloak. His wings became arms once more but, as he reached for the hammer, he felt a blow to the back of his head. A pair of frosty hands yanked him down into a dark hole, then everything went black.

Loki came to in a vast cavern, with his hands bound tightly behind his back. Icicles and stalagmites sparkled in the gloom. A shadowy figure sat hunched on a throne in front of him.

Loki shuddered as a blast of freezing giant breath hit the back of his neck. "Master," came a voice from behind, "look what I have brought – one of the hated Aesir gods."

"Fool!" bellowed the creature on the throne. "Don't you know this is Loki, the son of a giant. He may live in Asgard, but he is not a true Aesir."

"But master," whined the giant, "he came for the hammer, just as you planned..." His voice trailed off as the figure on the throne snapped his fingers. A guard stepped from the shadows and raised his sword. Loki watched in stunned silence as the guard sliced off the giant's head.

"Come closer, Loki," growled the voice from the throne. "Let me get a good look at you."

Loki stepped forward, to see a hideous frost giant, his body covered in jagged shards of ice. His eyes glowed red and narrowed into vicious slits as he smiled at Loki.

"I am Thrym, king of the frost giants," he said, "and you, Loki, are my prisoner."

"Please, noble king, let me go!" begged Loki. "I'll do anything you ask."

"Anything?" said Thrym. "Then bring me Freya, the beautiful Vanir goddess, so I can marry her and make her my queen."

"I will try, my lord."

"You will *succeed*, Loki! And then I'll return Mjollnir as part of the marriage ceremony. If you fail, neither you nor any of the Aesir will see this again!" And he taunted Loki by dangling the hammer before his eyes.

A guard cut through Loki's bonds, and he turned and ran. He found the falcon cloak on the ground where he'd landed, pulled it on and flew straight back to Asgard, grateful to be alive.

As Loki fluttered down to Freya's hall, he had already devised a plan. He was all the more pleased because he knew Thor would hate it.

"Well, Loki?" said Thor, the moment he saw him. "Have you found my hammer?"

"I have indeed," smiled Loki, "Mjollnir is in Jotunheim, just as I predicted."

"Then tell us," asked Freya, "which of those villainous frost giants has stolen it?"

"Thrym, their king," Loki replied. "He has Mjollnir in his underground palace."

"Well, what are we waiting for?" shouted Thor. "Let's go down and get it. I'm not afraid of frost giants, even their king!"

"We don't need to fight for it, Thor," said Loki. "Thrym says he'll give Mjollnir back to you, in return for a gift."

"What gift?" asked Thor.

"Freya's hand in marriage."

"For Odin's sake!" groaned Freya. "I will not be promised to such a revolting creature. I can't marry a frost giant – they're disgusting!"

"Don't worry," said Loki. "We're not actually going through with it. I've thought of a brilliant trick. Thor will pretend to be you. Thrym will return the hammer as part of the wedding ceremony."

"But how can I pretend to be Freya? I don't look anything like her."

"You'll be in a wedding dress, with a veil covering your face. Besides, to a frost giant, all gods look alike – they can barely tell us apart."

Thor scowled, but at least the plan meant he'd

get his Mjollnir back.

So Freya sewed together two of her finest gowns to make a wedding dress for Thor. She draped a veil over his face, and, as a final touch, gave him her necklace, Brisingamen, to wear.

"Thrym has never seen my face, but he must have heard about my fabulous necklace," boasted Freya.

After a long journey, Thor and Loki arrived at King Thrym's hall. Loki was convincingly disguised as a bridesmaid. Thor, on the other hand, hadn't even bothered to shave. But the frost

giants didn't notice.

"We'll begin with a feast," announced Thrym, smiling broadly at the veiled Thor. Servants brought out platters of the finest boar, deer and ox meat, and poured generous goblets of wine.

Loki, playing the part of a bridesmaid, ate daintily, but Thor didn't know how to act the blushing bride. He munched down two whole boars, one straight after the other, and belched.

Thrym was starting to get suspicious. Loki could see him muttering something to one of his guards. "O great and noble king," said Loki, in a high-pitched voice, "perhaps you've noticed a peculiar habit of Freya's. When she is happy, she needs to eat. And she's so excited about marrying you that she can't help but gorge herself."

"Ah, a woman after my own heart," chuckled

the king. "But if she's *that* excited, what are we waiting for? Let the wedding begin!"

He stood up and, with his mighty fists, flipped over the great feasting table, sending meat and drink flying. "The feast is over," he declared. "Now, bring me my bride so we can be married!"

Thor threw down a half-eaten ox leg and marched confidently towards Thrym. Even up close, Thrym didn't suspect a thing. He sat Thor down on a throne, and knelt before his bride-to-be. He placed Mjollnir on Thor's lap, then gently began to lift his veil. Thor held his breath.

Clutching the veil, Thrym stared in horror at the manly face beneath. "You!" he exclaimed. "You're not Freya, you're... you're..."

"I'm Thor!" yelled the thunder god.

He jumped up and swung Mjollnir down, again

and again, onto the thieving giant's head.

Thrym's spiky body began to crack, and Thor watched triumphantly as he shattered into a thousand icy splinters. Thor stomped on the shards, wielding his hammer threateningly. "No one comes between me and Mjollnir. NO ONE! Now, who's next?"

The other giants backed away, while Loki watched, an amused smile on his lips.

"Running won't do you any good!" Thor taunted. He lifted Mjollnir over his head and summoned the power of a storm. A tremendous bolt of lightning seared through the roof of the cave, setting fire to the overturned feast table.

"Come on, Thor," said Loki. "Let's get out of here before we burn to death!"

But Thor was in no hurry. He strode out of

Thor's Wedding Day

the cave, swirling his hammer, smashing giants left and right as he went, a savage grin spreading across his face.

Back in Asgard, Thor was expecting a hero's welcome. But instead, he found all the gods standing along the wall, pointing at him and laughing. The loudest sounds of all came from behind him. Thor whirled around to see Loki, bent double with laughter.

"What's the meaning of this, trickster?" Thor yelled, bearing down on Loki.

"Oh, Thor," replied Loki, between giggles, "take a look at yourself!"

Thor looked down. He was still wearing the wedding gown, only now its train was singed black from the fire, and the top was spattered with flecks of frost giant blood. A garland of frosty flowers had stuck to one of his boots and was trailing along the ground behind him.

"If you think about it," Loki added, with another splutter of laughter, "you could have recaptured your beloved hammer without dressing up at all!"

"You're right!" bellowed Thor. "Why did I ever listen to your wicked plan, you troll-eyed son of a worm. I could have easily killed Thrym and found my hammer without your so-called help. You just love making me look ridiculous."

"I do," said Loki, with a grin. "It's so much fun for the rest of us!"

Thor and the Frost Giants

Thor sighed when he spotted Loki lurking outside his window one morning. *He's probably up to another of his tricks,* Thor thought. This time, he was determined not to be the victim.

"What is it, Loki, you foul-smelling dragon-licker?" he shouted. "Have you come to make me look foolish again?"

"No, Thor, I don't have the energy to play tricks today. Please, just let me come in." Loki sounded weary, and Thor noticed a vicious cut running down his cheek.

"If you promise to behave yourself, I'll let you in," said Thor, sternly.

"I promise," Loki vowed.

"Good," said Thor. "Now, tell me what happened to your face?"

"It was that vile frost giant, Geirrod. I'd taken Freya's falcon cloak and was flying as a falcon over the mountains in Jotunheim, minding my own business..."

"I'll just bet you were," interrupted Thor.

"Anyway, I was tired, so I stopped for a rest on a quiet icy peak. How was I to know it was Geirrod's eyebrow I was standing on?"

"You mistook a giant's face for a mountain?" Thor exclaimed, roaring with laughter.

"You've never seen Geirrod, have you, Thor?" sneered Loki. "You wouldn't laugh if you could see how big he is. Why, even his daughters Gjalp and Greip are as big as Gladsheim!"

"Ha!" said Thor. "It's about time you fell for someone else's disguise, trickster. Go on with your sorry tale."

"Geirrod grabbed me with his massive hands, and chained me up in his dungeon. I've been trapped for days... Surely you noticed that I was missing?"

"I can't say I did."

"Well it doesn't matter, because I escaped!"

"And how did you manage that, a weakling like you against a frost giant as big as a mountain?"

"I used my brain, you buffoon – but maybe you don't have one?"

"Do you want my hammer to make a dent in your ugly head?" shouted Thor.

"You're such a bully!" retorted Loki. "Just like that brute, Geirrod. He's the one who cut my face, with his icy fingernails."

"How dare you compare me to a frost giant!" Thor snapped.

"You should be flattered," said Loki quickly. "I used your name, and your reputation, to help me escape."

"What do you mean?"

"I appealed to Geirrod's ego, which is nearly as big as he is. I told him that it was one thing to capture me, scrawny as I am, but he could never beat the mighty Thor in a fair fight."

"Well I'm sure that's true," declared Thor. "Just let me grab my hammer and I'll be happy to prove it to him!"

"Except..."

"Except what?"

"Mjollnir is such a powerful weapon, that it

wouldn't really be a fair fight if you used it."

"Maybe you're right. The day I can't defeat a frost giant with my bare fists is the day I stop calling myself the god of thunder!"

"Hooray for Thor!" cheered Loki. "Now get yourself off to Jotunheim, and show that fishbelly Geirrod what the Aesir are made of."

Spurred on by the thought of a heroic victory, Thor charged outside, leaving his precious hammer behind.

Loki smirked. *Thor is so easy to trick. He never guessed that I only escaped by promising Geirrod I would send Thor into Jotunheim without the protection of his hammer. I wonder how he'll get on...*

By the time Thor reached the foothills of the Jotunheim mountains, he was starting to feel the cold. He stopped in a cave for the night, cursing the snowy weather, and his own foolishness at not bringing a cloak.

Early the next morning, he was woken by a snarling sound. There, in the entrance to his cave, stood a gigantic bear. It was far larger and more savage than any bear found on Midgard. This one was capable of surviving the harsh Jotunheim winters and escaping the frost giants' snares.

Thor killed the creature with his bare hands, and cut off its skin to wear as a cloak. *That's better*, he thought. Ready to brave the weather, he stepped out of the cave and began the long, hard climb up the Jotunheim mountains.

Before long, Thor was lost in a thick blizzard.

In the distance he could make out a flickering light, and he trudged on through the swirling storm to reach it.

The light led him to a large wooden hut, half-covered by snow. Thor banged on a massive door and it creaked open. Inside, a giantess was bent over a stove, stirring a cooking pot. A rancid smell filled the cluttered hut, which was strewn with cauldrons, cobwebs and dusty piles of swords and shields.

The giantess looked down at Thor, showing her surprisingly beautiful face. "You are very far from home, little Aesir god," she said, smiling. "You must be tired and hungry. Come, sit at my table and taste my delicious soup."

Thor climbed up one of the tall stools next to the table and sat down.

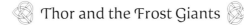

Peering into the pot, he saw a jumble of bones and even an eyeball, rolling around in the bubbling broth. Thor recoiled in disgust.

The giantess chuckled.

"Why should I trust you?" asked Thor, eyeing her suspiciously.

"I am Grid, a friend of Odin's," she replied. "I'm on your side. But tell me, what business do you have out here on the icy wastes of Jotunheim?"

"Revenge," snarled Thor. "I have come to repay the violence done to Loki, who was captured by that scoundrel, Geirrod."

"Geirrod?" Grid snapped. "He's more than

a scoundrel. Look at that magnificent ice hall," she went on, dragging Thor from his stool and holding him up to the window so he could see. "That was once my home. Geirrod and his daughters kicked me out the day after Odin came to visit me."

"After tomorrow, you need never worry about Geirrod again," Thor declared. "I've never lost a fight with a frost giant and I don't intend to start now."

"You arrogant god," said Grid. "Don't you know how big and powerful Geirrod is? Why, you barely come up to my waist, and Geirrod is at least twice my height."

"Only twice your height? That lying Loki! He told me Geirrod was as big as a mountain."

"Ha!" said Grid. "He's not that big, but he's

still too big for you to fight unarmed. Did you bring any weapons with you?"

"I don't need any weapons!"

"Maybe you don't and maybe you do," muttered Grid. "Now you eat some soup while I see what I can find that might help you." She headed to the back of the hut and began to rummage through the piles of junk.

Thor forced himself to drink the soup, and found that it warmed him and renewed his strength. He watched Grid sort through shields and helmets, swords and spears, sending them clattering across the floor.

At last, she produced a leather belt, a wooden staff and a pair of iron gloves. "These will do nicely," she said.

"Thank you," said Thor. "But how can they

help me? They're not weapons!"

"Use them and see," said Grid mysteriously. "Now, go and kill that monster!"

At Grid's words, Thor put on the belt and gloves, grabbed the staff and raced back out into the snow.

The blizzard had died down and he could see a path snaking down a slope to a river. On the far bank rose the great ice hall.

I'll bet Geirrod's inside, thought Thor. He pounded down the path and leaped onto the ice-covered river. But the ice was thin, and Thor fell into freezing water, right up to his waist. He forced his way forwards with gritted teeth.

Suddenly, he felt the water rising around him. It was almost up to his armpits when he heard a horrible screeching laugh from the bank.

There, grinning down at the god, was a gnarled and ugly frost giantess.

"You must be one of Geirrod's revolting daughters," taunted Thor. "Which one are you, Gjalp or Greip?"

"I'm Gjalp. And I may be ugly, but at least I don't smell like a boar's behind!" The frost giantess howled with laughter. She was holding a tree over the river and shaking it violently.

Icicles rained down onto Thor, melting into the river and filling it higher and higher.

Thor looked around desperately for something to throw at her. All he could see was a boulder nearly twice his size. Even with his tremendous strength, he doubted he'd be able to lift it.

But he could think of nothing else. Thor waded over to the boulder and grasped it firmly.

At that moment, he felt a burst of energy surge through his body. It was coming from the belt Grid had given him. Thor looked down at it in wonder, then hurled the boulder.

It smashed into Gjalp, shattering her into thousands of tiny pieces.

Struggling out of the river, Thor abandoned his sodden bearskin cloak and stormed into the hall. His footsteps echoed on the icy floor. The place seemed deserted. All he could see was a vast table, with a small chair at one end.

Wondering what to do next, Thor sat down on the chair – only to feel it move. A frosty head appeared at his feet.

"Enjoy the ride!" chuckled Greip, starting to stand, the chair wedged on top of her icy head.

"If she stands up to her full height, I'll be

squashed into
the ceiling like a
fly!" Thor realized.
As he rose into the
air, he quickly lodged
the wooden staff
between the seat of
the chair and the
ceiling. Greip pushed
hard against it...

There was a sharp crack and Thor dropped
to the ground.

Greip's neck had broken. The giantess had
killed herself trying to snap the magical staff.

Only one enemy remained – Geirrod
himself. At that moment, the giant stomped
through the doorway, lugging a cauldron. Inside,

were gigantic lumps of coal, each the size of Thor's head, and glowing red hot. Using a pair of tongs, Geirrod plucked out a coal and flung it over the table, right at Thor's face.

Thor ducked the flying rock, only to find a second, then a third, hurtling his way. He just managed to dodge them, though the heat singed his hair as they shot past. Quickly, he put on the iron gloves that Grid had given him and grabbed the nearest coal. The gloves glowed red but Thor couldn't feel the heat on his hands.

Without waiting a moment longer, he flung the coal at Geirrod. For all his vast size, the giant was quick on his feet. He dodged the coal and darted behind a pillar.

Thor narrowed his eyes and picked up another piece of coal. Summoning all his strength, he sent it crashing into the pillar – so hard, it punched right through and smashed into Geirrod's face, melting a hole in his icy brain.

The frost giant collapsed to the floor, and Thor stood on top of his vanquished enemy, beating his chest with pride. "I, Thor, am the mightiest of all!" he shouted to the empty hall.

Armed with his new staff, gloves and belt, Thor strode out of the hall and headed home, picking as many fights as possible along the way.

He returned to Asgard, his head swollen with pride, bragging to all the gods that he'd defeated not one, but three enormous frost giants – all without using his hammer.

Loki scowled. Even when tricked into an unarmed battle, the thunder god had come out on top.

STORIES OF GIANTS

Ever since Odin and his brothers had killed Ymir, the first king of the frost giants, nearly every giant in Jotunheim had hated the Aesir gods. The giants seized any chance offered to challenge the gods and take their revenge...

Hrungnir Against the Gods

Hrungnir the stone giant was sitting outside his cave in Jotunheim, gouging great lumps of rock out of the ground. Soon, he had a towering pile. "These will be perfect for hurling at gods," he chuckled.

At the sound of hoofbeats he looked up, a grim smile on his face as he recognized Odin, Allfather of the Aesir. "How dare you show your face in Jotunheim, you one-eyed sneak!" Hrungnir shouted, flinging a rock at him.

Odin ducked and charged forward, the rock passing harmlessly over his head. Hrungnir grabbed another rock and threw again.

"I can keep dodging rocks all day," said Odin. "But why are you throwing them at me?"

"You arrogant gods need to learn that you can't come to Jotunheim without paying a price," Hrungnir snarled.

"We Aesir go where we please," retorted Odin, looking the giant square in the eyes. "We can outfight, outthink and even outrun the best of you! My horse, Sleipnir, is the fastest in the nine realms. You couldn't catch me if you tried." And with that, Odin thumbed his nose at Hrungnir, turned his horse and sped off back up the mountainside.

"You won't get away from me that easily!" cried the giant. He put his fingers in his cavernous mouth and whistled. Immediately, a fine stallion trotted up.

"Go, Gullfaxi!" Hrungnir roared at his horse, swinging himself up and charging past Odin.

At the top of the mountain, Hrungnir stopped and sneered. "Ha! My Gullfaxi is a thousand times faster than your puny eight-legged spider-pony."

"Oh, so it's a race you're after?" taunted Odin. "If you want to see how fast Sleipnir can really go, hold tight to your horse's mane. We don't slow down for hills, or forests, not even for great, flowing rivers."

Hrungnir grunted, and the race was on.

At first, Gullfaxi pulled ahead of Sleipnir. He knew the mountain paths of Jotunheim well. But Odin wasn't worried. They were fast approaching a vast ocean, where he was sure he would take the lead. Sleipnir had a secret – he could fly.

Odin urged Sleipnir on, up and over a cliff, and together they soared into the sky. Looking back, Odin laughed to see Hrungnir and Gullfaxi plummeting into the waves below.

But his laughter stopped abruptly as the giant and his steed rose out of the sea. Gullfaxi's legs created a great blur of motion, working so fast that his hooves skipped across the water.

Eventually, the ocean gave way to land, and the race continued across the fields and forests of Midgard. It was dusk by the time Odin and Hrungnir galloped up to the foot of Bifrost, the rainbow bridge.

Heimdall, the guardian of Asgard, saw the two riders approaching over the bridge. "Come on, Odin!" he shouted. "You can't lose to that ugly rock-faced monster!"

The pair were neck-and-neck as they reached the gate of Asgard. "Odin! Odin!" chanted the gods, who had gathered along the walls to watch.

But Hrungnir refused to give in.

Gullfaxi matched Sleipnir stride for stride, until the two horses came skidding to a halt at the doors of Valhalla itself. There was nowhere for the competitors to go. The race was over – in a dead heat.

"Well done, Hrungnir!" said Odin, extending a hand to his opponent. "You nearly beat me!"

"Even though you cheated by racing on a flying horse!" said Hrungnir, knocking Odin's hand away.

"Are you going to argue with me here, outside my own hall?" demanded Odin.

Hrungnir dismounted and looked around, realizing for the first time that he was trapped deep in the realm of his enemies. "You tricked me!" he shouted at Odin. "You led me here on purpose so you could murder me."

Odin stared into Hrungnir's eyes, enjoying the giant's look of fear. But then his own eye twinkled, and the sides of his mouth lifted in a broad grin. "Now is not the time to fight," he declared. "It's time for a feast! A feast to celebrate the greatest race that was ever run."

Hrungnir stumbled through the doors of Valhalla and sat down warily. He couldn't quite believe Odin's words. He called for a goblet of mead and gulped it down. "I'll say this for you Aesir, you know how to mix fine mead! Now bring me food – and plenty of it." The gods laughed and sat down to join him.

But as the evening turned into night, Hrungnir's hatred for the Aesir resurfaced. He started flinging insults at his hosts. "You sneaky gods with your dirty tricks! You thought you could trap me here in Asgard, didn't you? Well let me tell you, I can outfight any of you. In fact, I'd win even if you all attacked at the same time!"

"You watch your mouth!" said Thor.

"And another thing," Hrungnir went on, with

a loud belch, "you think you can buy me off with a sip of mead and a few measly roast boar? Call this a feast? More like chicken feed!"

"But you were just saying how much you liked the mead," protested Tyr, god of war.

"I was being polite," snapped Hrungnir, dashing his goblet on the ground.

"How dare you!" shouted Thor, rising to his feet and snarling at the giant. "You'd better pick that up and apologize, or else!"

"Or else what?"

"Or else you'll feel my hammer smashing your ugly face to smithereens!"

The Aesir were all on their feet, fists punching the air and chanting, "Fight! Fight! Fight!"

Hrungnir swung a fist at Thor. But he lost his balance and toppled forward. Thor tried to hit back, and was caught by the falling giant. The pair landed in a tangled heap on the floor.

Tyr helped them onto their chairs. "Tonight you both need to sleep," he said. "You can finish your fight tomorrow."

"Agreed," mumbled Thor. "Let's meet outside the gates of Asgard at dawn..."

The next morning, Hrungnir woke up, washed his stony face with a handful of gravel, and raced to meet Thor. All the Aesir had gathered along Asgard's wall to watch the impending battle. In the crowd, Hrungnir could see Thor's young son, Magni, smiling and waving. But there was no sign of Thor.

"Where is he?" Hrungnir taunted angrily. "Has that coward decided to hide? Let me at him so I can crush his feeble bones!"

Thor burst open the gates. "Here I am, flint-face. Do your worst!"

Standing up to his full height, Hrungnir was nearly twice as tall as Thor. "You think you can hurt me, flesh-thing?" he mocked. "Show me your weapon."

Thor held out his hammer, Mjollnir.

"Ho, ho, ho!" laughed the giant. "You'll never harm me with that tiny thing." He bent down to the ground and lifted up a huge stone slab. It was almost as big as Thor.

"Your rock may be large, but you'll have to hit me with it first," goaded Thor. And he began to back away.

"That's right, run away, little god," teased Hrungnir. "But don't think that will save you!"

Thor stopped, a look of anger on his face. "I'm not running away, you fool! I'm just giving myself space... to do this!"

He swung back his arm, then flung Mjollnir through the air. The giant just had time to throw his stone at the hammer, hoping to block it.

But Mjollnir was simply too powerful. It smashed the stone slab into pieces and kept on going. Hrungnir's eyes widened in fear, then went dead as the hammer punched right through his stone heart.

Thor ducked as shards of flint flew through the air. One of the shards drilled into his forehead and he cried out in pain. But the real danger

was still to come. Hrungnir was falling to the ground. Thor tried to run, but there was nowhere to go...

...and the mountainous giant crashed on top of him. Thor was trapped. He desperately tried to shove the monster away, but the dead weight of Hrungnir was too much. Tyr and Balder raced down from the wall to help, but even the three Aesir together weren't strong enough to lift the giant.

"Father, what's the matter?" called Thor's son, Magni, from the crowd. "Why don't you come out?"

"I'm stuck, son," Thor grunted in reply.

"But it's only a little giant," said Magni, jumping off the wall. He crouched down and put his hands under Hrungnir's massive chest.

The watching crowd gasped as the child lifted the giant high above his head.

Thor crawled out from underneath and hugged his son. "How strong you've become, young Magni!" he said proudly. "One day, you will grow up to be an even greater warrior than your father. Here, you should take Hrungnir's horse, Gullfaxi.

Hrungnir won't be needing him any more!"

The Aesir cheered, and Thor basked in the glory of another famous victory, another giant defeated. But although Hrungnir had lost his life, he had won a measure of revenge against the gods. From that moment on, every time Thor went into battle, he felt a searing pain from the piece of flint that had lodged in his brain.

Thiazi and
the Golden Apples

Thiazi the giant lived on a high mountain at the far-flung edge of Jotunheim. On clear days, he transformed himself into an eagle, swooping as close to the walls of Asgard as he dared. On soaring wings, he spied on the gods below, watching and listening, until he uncovered a secret so powerful, he hoped it would bring down the gods themselves...

In a little corner of Asgard, he'd spotted a beautiful orchard. And in the middle of that

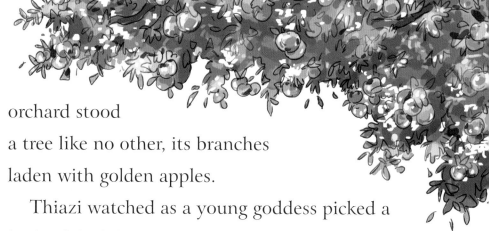

orchard stood
a tree like no other, its branches
laden with golden apples.

Thiazi watched as a young goddess picked a basketful of the apples, then gave one to each of the gods to eat. Almost instantly, the gods began to shimmer with a golden glow. *Those apples are magical,* thought Thiazi. *I must taste one for myself!*

He sat and waited for one of the gods to leave the safety of Asgard. He didn't have to wait long. The very next day, Odin, his brother Honir, and Loki came ambling down the rainbow bridge.

"Remember to get into your disguises before we reach Midgard," said Odin. "We don't want to startle any humans we might encounter!"

Thiazi watched the trio put on old hunting cloaks and hats. He took on his eagle form and followed them as they entered Midgard. When the gods eventually stopped to rest, Thiazi hid himself in the branches of a tree.

"I'm hungry," Honir complained.

"You and your stomach!" said Loki. "All you ever talk about is food. But if it'll keep you quiet, let's eat that boar over there."

Loki killed the boar with ease, then brought it over to Honir. "Well, aren't you going to help me cook it, lazy bones?" demanded Loki.

"You cook it, Loki," ordered Odin. "After all, my brother and I are your elders and betters."

The two gods laughed while Loki set to work, mouthing silent curses at his companions. He quickly made a fire, and soon had the boar carcass roasting on a spit above it.

"Isn't the food cooked yet?" Honir grumbled,

coming over to inspect the meat.

"I don't understand," said Loki, hacking off a piece with his knife. "It's still raw."

"Don't play the fool with me, Loki!" stormed Odin. "This is one of your tricks."

"I swear this isn't a trick," protested Loki. "At least, it's no trick of *my* doing."

At that moment, Thiazi flew down from his perch. "Loki is right," he called. "It's not *his* fault the boar isn't cooking – it's *mine*!"

"Wretched bird!" shouted Honir, trying to bash the eagle with his club. "What foul magic is this? How dare you keep me from my supper!" But the bird easily flew out of his reach.

"I'll make you a deal," said Thiazi. "If you let me have the first bite, I'll undo my spell."

"I don't trust him," hissed Loki.

"I'm still hungry," Honir muttered back. "Let's just agree so we can eat."

Odin gave a nod and Thiazi breathed onto the fire, which roared and crackled in response. Soon, the boar was cooking beautifully.

"Remember, I get the first bite," called Thiazi.

When the meat was done, he swooped onto the boar, gnawing at it with his powerful beak while the others looked on in envy.

Then, without warning, he began to beat his enormous wings, taking to the air with the boar clutched in his talons.

"Thieving bird!" Odin howled in rage.

Loki picked up his staff and thrust it as hard as he could at Thiazi. The staff stuck fast to the bird's side, but Thiazi kept beating his wings and soared ever upward, taking Loki with him.

"Let go, you fool!" Odin called out.

"I can't," shouted Loki. "That wicked bird is using magic to bind my hand to the stick."

Thiazi cackled and swooped down low over a thorn bush. Loki screamed in pain as he was dragged through the thorns.

"Let me go!" he demanded.

Thiazi cackled once more, flying on to a distant cliff top. He landed at the very edge of the cliff, with Loki dangling above the sea.

"I'll set you free if you make me a promise."

"Anything!" begged Loki, staring in horror at the churning waves.

"I want to eat one of your golden apples."

"But I don't have any! Idunn, the goddess who tends the orchard, keeps them all."

"Then bring Idunn and her apples to me."

Loki hesitated, and Thiazi took off again, threatening to drag Loki through the thorn bush once more. "No, please, let me go!" Loki cried. "I'll do it. Wait for me at the bottom of Bifrost, and I'll bring Idunn to you."

"You'd better," said Thiazi. He released Loki, letting him drop to the ground, then flew away.

Muttering curses, Loki hobbled back to his companions.

"What happened to you?" Honir asked.

"That beastly bird dragged me through the prickliest bush and the sharpest stones he could find," whined Loki. "But I managed to break his spell. He flew off before I could teach him a lesson, though."

"Is that *really* what happened?" asked Odin.

"Would I lie to you?" Loki replied.

"Yes!" said Odin and Honir together. "But never mind that now," continued Honir. "Let's go home to Asgard and get something to eat."

But Loki wasn't hungry. As the others headed off to eat, he crept over to the orchard.

"Sweet, beautiful Idunn," he began. "You are a kind goddess. Won't you take pity on a poor bruised wretch, and let me have one of your apples to heal my aching body?"

Idunn smiled and brought out a basket of apples. She loved to watch the gods eat her apples, to see their youth and happiness return as the magical fruit restored their bodies.

She was so entranced watching Loki's face that

she didn't notice him stealing a second apple from her basket.

"Thank you, Idunn," said Loki, wiping syrupy juice from his lips. "Do you know, while I was in Midgard I found a tree with its own golden apples, just like yours." He dropped the stolen apple from his sleeve and gave it to Idunn.

"But that's impossible," she declared.

"Let me show you," said Loki. "Bring your basket of apples and come with me. We can compare yours to the ones from the tree in Midgard. Wouldn't it be terrible if humans discovered the secret of eternal life?"

Filled with curiosity, Idunn agreed, and the pair set off down the rainbow bridge to Midgard. But no sooner had they arrived, than Thiazi swept down on them, claws outstretched. He snatched Idunn and her basket, then soared back up into the sky.

Loki filled his voice with false fury. "Come back, you scoundrel!" he called, pretending to leap after the bird, his fist raised.

"The apples!" Idunn cried from above. "What will you do without them?"

But as soon as Idunn had disappeared over the hills, Loki allowed himself to smile. *I'll miss Idunn and her apples*, he thought, *but won't it be fun seeing what happens now that she's away...*

At first, the gods of Asgard didn't even notice Idunn was missing. But then, as the weeks passed by, they began to feel old and weary. Worse, they began to fall sick – and no god had ever been sick before.

"Frigg, help me," Odin sniffed through a

runny nose. "Use your magic healing powers to cure this strange affliction."

"I wish I could," replied Frigg, "but I'm so tired all the time. My legs feel so heavy I can barely move, let alone cast a spell. What we really need is one of Idunn's golden apples."

"But where is she?" moaned Thor. "Oh, if only I had the strength to lift my hammer, I'd smash my way out of this mess."

"It wouldn't help," grumbled Frey. "Some problems need brains, not brawn."

"Speaking of brains," Honir chimed in, "where's Loki? He's the only one who has managed to get up and leave the hall."

"Loki! Loki!" chorused the gods in hoarse, wheezing voices. They had to wait a long time before Loki came back into the hall.

"What's the matter?" Loki asked.

"You must find Idunn, Loki," called Odin. "We need her golden apples to restore our youth."

"I wonder where she could be," mused Loki.

"I think Loki knows exactly where Idunn is," muttered Thor, as he watched Loki leave. "We'd better try to follow him."

But Loki had vanished. He was the last to eat an apple, and he still had the energy to skip to Freya's house, steal her falcon cloak and fly away.

Loki headed straight to Thiazi's mountain hall, where he found Idunn in a high tower, all alone.

"You rotten scoundrel!" she cried. "Thiazi told

me how you helped him to kidnap me."

Loki laughed dismissively. "Come now, is that any way to talk to your rescuer?"

Just then, Loki and Idunn heard footsteps outside. Thiazi burst into the room as Loki cast a spell that transformed Idunn... into a nut.

Loki grabbed her in his falcon claws and dived out of the window, beating his wings hard. But in an instant, Thiazi the eagle was after him, a sharp beak snapping at his falcon tail.

"Fly, little falcon," taunted Thiazi. "I'll catch you, and then I'll kill you!"

Loki knew he couldn't outfly the eagle. Like the other gods, weakness and sickness were finally creeping up on him. He flapped his aching wings harder, desperate to reach Asgard.

By the time he could see the wall, Thiazi was

looming above him. Loki shouted to the gods who were watching, "Make a fire! And hurry!"

The Aesir summoned the last of their strength to build a pile of burning wood on Asgard's wall. Loki swooped over the flickering flames, just in time... As Thiazi followed, the flames leaped in the air, catching at his wings.

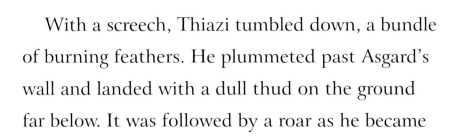

With a screech, Thiazi tumbled down, a bundle of burning feathers. He plummeted past Asgard's wall and landed with a dull thud on the ground far below. It was followed by a roar as he became a giant once more. "I'll get you, gods!" he fumed.

"Oh no you won't," said Thor. He hoisted his hammer over the wall and it fell with a deadly smack on Thiazi's head.

Loki dropped the nut into Frigg's hands, and everyone cheered when it transformed into Idunn, still clutching her basket of apples. One by one, she gave them to the gods, restoring their health and their beauty. Loki was last of all. She held an apple out to him – then paused.

"I'm not sure you deserve this, Loki," she said.

"Of course I do," he retorted. "After all, I did rescue you. All of you, in fact."

The gods roared in anger but Loki was too quick. "I'll see you later, when you've had a chance to see the funny side," he taunted, snatching the apple and running off to hide.

Lost in the Land of the Giants

"Hey, Loki, where are you off to?" yelled Thor, as he watched Loki climbing over the great wall of Asgard.

"Shh!" hissed Loki. "I'm going into Jotunheim to spy on the frost giants – I think they're up to something. But there's no point if you shout it so loudly their guards can hear."

"I don't believe you!" said Thor. "Every time you go into Jotunheim, you make trouble for me. I bet you're going to plot some tricks with the giants."

"How dare you doubt my loyalty to Asgard! Haven't I always helped you beat the frost giants?"

"Even if you're right, I still don't trust you!"

snapped Thor. "I'm coming with you. And we're not going to sneak around, either. Wait there."

A few moments later, Thor came thundering by on his chariot, his goats Toothgnasher and Toothgrinder champing at the bit. "Jump on, Loki – unless you think you can keep up with me on foot!"

Loki leaped onto the chariot, Thor cracked his whip and together they sped off to Jotunheim.

They rode the chariot for a whole day, but didn't find a single giant. "Bah!" grumbled Thor. "I thought I'd have fought at least ten giants by now. And I'm hungry. Let's find somewhere to stop for the night."

"There's a hut over there," suggested Loki. But as he spoke, the goats gave a loud bleat and reared up. Thor and Loki were flung from the chariot. Thor sprang to his feet, hammer in hand, only to see a young boy in front of him.

"Where did you come from, little boy?" he boomed angrily.

"From my house over there," said the boy.

"And what's a human child doing in Jotunheim?" Loki asked, suspiciously.

"Jotunheim?" said the boy. "We're not in Jotunheim. This is Utgard – the outlands."

"Curses!" cried Thor. "We're not even in the right place. And who might you be?"

"Thialfi the swift," replied the boy proudly.

"Ha! *Thialfi the swift*," mocked Thor. "I bet you're not as fast as my two fine goats here."

"How about a race? From here to my house," said Thialfi, pointing to the hut in the distance.

"I never back down from a challenge," said Thor. "And I never lose, either!"

Thor and Loki took their places in the chariot and the race was on. Thialfi sprinted into the lead. Thor spurred his goats forward, but he couldn't catch the boy. When they reached the hut, Thialfi wasn't even out of breath.

"Cheat!" said Thor. "I wasn't ready. That race doesn't count."

"Ignore him," said Loki, chuckling. "Thor is

just a sore loser."

"Harrumph!" Thor snorted. "I'll beat you yet, Thialfi. First, though, I need food and rest. What can you offer two starving guests?"

"You're very welcome to sleep here, but my family has no food. The giants of Utgard have stolen everything from us."

"If you have no food, we'll have to use our emergency rations," said Thor. He took his hammer, and slammed it onto Toothgnasher's head, killing the goat instantly. Then he struck Toothgrinder, too.

"What are you doing?" asked Loki.

"Making supper! Don't worry, the goats will be fine in the morning."

Thor is a simpleton, thought Loki, *but even he can't be as simple as that, surely?*

Thor cooked the two goats and everyone ate heartily. "Just be careful not to break the bones," Thor said. "Now, I'm off to bed. Good night."

But Thialfi hadn't eaten this well for weeks. He couldn't resist. He waited until the others were asleep, then broke open Toothgrinder's thigh bone, and sucked out the marrow. *Thor won't notice if I put it back together,* he thought.

The next morning, Thor gathered all the bones and placed them in two separate piles. He stood between them, swirling Mjollnir over his head. The hammer whirled with such speed, a great wind whipped the bones into the air.

Loki and Thialfi looked on in wonder, as the spinning bones took on new flesh and hair, and the goats gradually re-formed. The pair bleated with the shock of their strange rebirth, but then smiled in triumph as they stretched their legs and walked around.

"What's this?" roared Thor with anger. "Why is Toothgrinder limping? Somebody broke a bone, I know it!"

"It was me," said Thialfi, cowering on his knees. "How can I make it up to you?"

"From now on, you will be my servant."

"Forever?" gulped Thialfi.

"Forever," repeated Thor, hoisting the boy into his chariot. Then, with a crack of the whip, they were off once more.

Oddly, a second day's journey brought them no

closer to the frost giants. "Where are they?" Thor complained, once they'd stopped for the night. "I need to hit something, and soon!"

"I don't understand it," said Loki. "We should be in Jotunheim by now."

"Are you telling me we're lost, Loki?" asked Thor, annoyed.

"No," said Loki, glaring at Thor. "But it's getting dark, and I think we should rest. We can work out a plan in the morning."

"And then we can fight some frost giants?"

"Yes, Thor, tomorrow we'll find you a nice, big giant to hit."

"Come and see!" Thialfi called from up ahead. "I've found a cave where we can sleep."

"How strange," commented Thor as they walked around it. "It has five separate chambers."

"Perfect," Loki teased. "I won't have to sleep next to you, Thor. You snore like a dwarf."

The cave floor was soft and surprisingly comfortable but, the next morning, Thor, Loki and Thialfi woke to feel the cave tilting up towards the sky.

"What's happening?" asked Thor, in a panic. "Why is the ground moving?"

Before anyone could answer, all three of them tumbled out of the cave and landed with a thump on the ground.

"By Odin's all-seeing eye!" Thor cried, pointing to the sky. "Look at that!"

Loki and Thialfi looked up to see a giant so tall his head touched the clouds. In his hand, casting a long shadow over them, was a gigantic glove.

"That glove was our cave!" exclaimed Thialfi.

The giant yawned and stretched his arms wide, blocking out the sun. "I am the giant Skrymir," he said. "And who are you?" he added, bending down for a closer look.

"I am Thor, god of thunder," bellowed Thor.

"Speak up," said Skrymir, his bearded face looming over Thor's. "I can't hear you."

"BEWARE! I AM THOR!" the god shouted, at the top of his voice.

"But you're so tiny," said Skrymir. "I can't believe any giant could be scared of you."

"Oh no?" Thor retorted. "Well let me show you why I am feared throughout Jotunheim." He hoisted himself up on the giant's beard, and climbed his craggy face. When he reached the top of the giant's head, he brought down Mjollnir with a crashing blow.

"See, Thor," laughed Loki, "I told you we'd find you a nice big giant to hit."

But Thor wasn't laughing. His hammer blow had barely dented the giant's head.

"Did you swat a fly off my head?" asked Skrymir, brushing Thor to the ground. "That's very kind of you."

"My mightiest blow, compared to someone swatting a fly? How can this be?"

"Do not take it to heart, little god," said Skrymir. "We giants of the outlands are *far* more powerful than those frosty upstarts in Jotunheim.

Come, I'll show you the way to the hall of my king, Utgardaloki."

"Slow down!" called Loki, as Skrymir strode ahead – but it was too late. Skrymir's long legs had already carried him far into the distance.

"I'll catch up with him," said Thialfi, eager to impress. He took off at a terrific sprint, but even he couldn't keep up. Skrymir's every step measured a mile.

Thor and Loki followed in the chariot, and eventually they arrived outside a great hall. Skrymir was nowhere to be seen. Instead, at the entrance, they saw Thialfi standing beside an elegantly dressed giant, only a head or two taller than Thor.

"I am Utgardaloki, king of Utgard," he said. "Welcome to my hall. Please, come inside. You are my guests."

"I don't trust him, Thor," hissed Loki. "A giant, being nice... it has to be a trick."

"Don't be such a coward, Loki," Thor whispered back. "Even if this is a trick, I can always smash my way out with Mjollnir!"

"And that worked out so well against Skrymir," Loki pointed out sarcastically.

"What's this?" interrupted Utgardaloki. "Are you arguing with each other? Please, put aside your squabbles and come inside to eat."

"Proper food at last!" said Thor. He followed Utgardaloki to a huge table laden with food, and helped himself to a plate of roast boar.

Loki sat next to Thor, sniffing the food on his plate suspiciously. "How do we know this isn't poisoned?" he asked.

"Ah, Loki," said Utgardaloki, "a perfectly reasonable question coming from a trickster like you. But I assure you, the food here is good to eat." To prove the point, he took a hunk of bread from Loki's own plate and ate it himself.

"The food is excellent, Loki," mumbled Thor through a mouthful of meat. "And everyone in Asgard knows you have the biggest appetite – although it doesn't show on your feeble frame."

"What's this?" asked Utgardaloki. "Is it true, Loki, that you are a champion eater?"

"Well, I'm not one to brag," replied Loki, lying shamelessly. "But yes, it so happens I am."

"Excellent – we shall have a contest! Wait here." Utgardaloki stepped through a doorway, and returned with a short giant, only a little larger than Loki. "This is Logi," he said. "He is

Utgard's champion eater."

Logi took a seat at the far end of the table, opposite his opponent. Utgardaloki summoned his servants, who piled the table high with bread, meat, cheese and fruit. Loki smiled, full of confidence.

"Let the contest begin!" declared Utgardaloki.

Loki chomped his way through four loaves of bread and three roasted oxen before looking up to check on his opponent. He couldn't believe it – Logi had devoured every last crumb.

"How..?" started Loki, before falling into a stunned silence.

"Ha!" laughed Utgardaloki. "No one is a match for Logi!"

"Arrogant scoundrel!" cried Thor. "I am an Aesir, and I am a match for anyone!"

"Perhaps *you* have a skill you'd like to test, Thor?" asked the giant king, rubbing his hands with glee.

"I have a powerful thirst," declared Thor. "I challenge you giants to a drinking contest."

"Well, there is no one to answer your challenge," said Utgardaloki, "but I can still arrange a little test of your prowess." He snapped his fingers and two servants brought out the biggest drinking horn Thor had ever seen.

"No giant has ever managed to drain this horn completely. Think you can do it, Thor?"

"Simple," said Thor, grabbing it eagerly. For long minutes, he gulped from the horn. But when at last he set it down, it was nearly as full as before.

"What?" cried Thor. "That's not possible!" And he drank again, longer and deeper. He drank until his belly felt fit to burst, but still the horn was almost full. Thor's face turned purple with rage, and he let out an almighty roar. "This... cannot... be!" he shouted.

"Let *me* challenge a giant," Thialfi piped up. "I can't eat or drink like a god, but I can outrun anybody – at least, anybody my own size."

"Is that so, young human?" said Utgardaloki. "Perhaps you'd care to test your speed against Hugi here? Shall we say, two laps of the hall?"

Thialfi turned to Hugi. *He doesn't look like a sprinter,* thought Thialfi. *I bet I can beat him.*

Utgardaloki gave a signal, and the two set off.

Hugi finished before Thialfi was even halfway through his first lap. Embarrassed, Thialfi hid behind Loki and Thor.

"I just don't understand it," said Thor. "How can we have lost every challenge? We must defend the name of Asgard. Utgardaloki, I demand a test of strength. My muscles have never failed me!"

"Very well, Thor," said the giant king. "Here is a challenge I'm sure you'll find very easy. Lift my cat above your head."

A black cat jumped out from beneath Utgardaloki's chair and slunk towards Thor. He grabbed the cat around its waist and tried to lift it. With every sinew straining, Thor managed to raise one of the cat's paws off the ground, before collapsing in an exhausted heap on the floor.

"This is intolerable!" growled Thor. "Give me someone I can fight, loathsome king, before I bring this entire hall down around you!"

"Let me go easy on you, Thor," replied Utgardaloki. "You must be tired after all your exertions." He beckoned to an elderly woman in the corner, who shuffled towards them. "This is Elli, who nursed me when I was a child. If you can wrestle her to the ground, I'll acknowledge that you Aesir are worthy foes."

"I wouldn't normally fight an old woman," said Thor, "but I'm so angry, I'll make an exception, just this once." He wrapped his arms around the woman and started to squeeze. At first, he seemed to be winning, as Elli's knees shook. But then she grabbed his shoulders with her bony hands, and applied such pressure that it was Thor's turn to buckle.

He went down on one knee, pushing against the crone with all his might, the veins in his forehead bulging with the strain. But he couldn't hold out forever...

"Enough!" Thor shouted at last. "I give in."

Utgardaloki nodded at Elli, who let go of
Thor. The defeated god shuffled over to Loki
and Thialfi, who both looked astonished to see
the mighty Thor laid low by an old woman
and a cat.

"Let's leave this unholy place," said Thor, "and
never tell anyone what happened here!"

"Before you leave, you must make me a

promise," said Utgardaloki ominously.

"What promise?" demanded Thor.

"You must promise that the gods of Asgard will never attack the giants of Utgard. It is no great request. After all, have you not learned that to challenge us would lead only to defeat?"

Scowling, Thor and Loki placed their hands on Utgardaloki's. "By Odin and Frigg, Allfather and Allmother of Asgard, we swear never to attack," they intoned solemnly.

Dejected, the trio trudged out of the hall and into the mists of Utgard. They climbed back into Thor's chariot, and were about to speed off when Utgardaloki appeared in front of them.

"Wait!" he commanded. "Since you've made your promise, I'll reveal the truth."

"The truth?" asked Loki.

"Yes," replied the king. "All was not as it seemed, for I, Utgardaloki, King of Utgard, am a master of illusions."

"Explain yourself," demanded Thor.

"I first cast a spell to make the cave you slept in appear to be a gigantic glove. Then I took on the guise of Skrymir, an impossibly tall giant.

"In my hall, my champion eater Logi was not a giant at all, but *fire* – the greatest devourer of all. And you, fleet-footed Thialfi, raced against another illusion. Hugi was *thought*, brought to life. Loki and Thialfi, that you managed even to compete is testament to your power."

Thialfi smiled, his spirits lifted a little, but Loki was deep in thought. *If these giants can wield such powerful magic, maybe I should switch my loyalty to them...*

"What about my challenges?" asked Thor. "What tricks did you dare to play on me?"

"You, Thor, have nothing to be ashamed of," said Utgardaloki. "The horn you drank from drew its liquid from the great ocean that surrounds Midgard. And my cat was no cat at all – it was Jormungand, the world serpent.

"Most impressive of all was your ability to hold your own against Elli, who was old age itself. Even gods must age and die eventually, but you, Thor, fought valiantly against her.

"Power and skills such as yours would surely bring the Aesir victory in battle against the giants of Utgard. But now we are safe, protected by your promise!" Utgardaloki opened his mouth wide and laughed heartily.

"Curse you, wicked giant!" Thor hissed

through his teeth. "We promised not to return, but we're still here and I can still hit you!" He raised his hammer and swung it at the king... but the hammer passed harmlessly through him. Loki, Thor and Thialfi could only watch as the king dissolved into the mist, which cleared away to reveal neither the weird wilds of Utgard nor the frozen wastes of Jotunheim, but the green fields of Asgard.

"What trickery is this?" asked Thor, as he led Thialfi and Loki back to his hall. "Were we ever in the Land of the Giants at all?"

"Who knows?" Loki shrugged. "But with magic that powerful, I don't think we should ever go back."

THE GOLDEN CURSE

The gods of Asgard loved to visit Midgard, the realm of men. They came seeking adventure but all too often what they found was trouble. On one such trip, a trio of careless gods set in motion a terrible chain of events, wreaking havoc with cursed gold, a deadly dragon and one man's desperate desire for revenge.

The Otter's Ransom

The waterfall glimmered in the sun as Loki, Honir and Odin stopped to admire the view.

"What a lovely day to explore Midgard," said Odin. "I knew it would be," he added, with a benevolent smile. "I had Thor put away his hammer so there'd be no thunderstorms to spoil our walk."

But Loki's mind wasn't on the weather. *By the position of the sun,* he thought, as he looked up, *it must be nearly lunchtime. Good! I'm starving.*

He inspected the rocks around the waterfall, hoping to spot something to eat. "Look at that otter!" he said to his companions, pointing to where it sat on a rock. "And, more importantly, look at that delicious fish it has in its mouth." He picked up a stone. "I bet I can kill the otter with one strike and bag us that salmon."

"I bet you can't," Odin scoffed. "You throw like a mortal, Loki!"

"Nonsense!" said Loki. He hadn't been sure if he could be bothered to kill the otter to retrieve the fish, but now he *had* to do it.

He lobbed the stone and hit the otter smack between the eyes. It slumped forward, dead, with the salmon still clutched between its teeth.

"Dinner AND an otterskin with one stone," crowed Loki. He did a little dance of triumph.

"Throw like a mortal? Mortals will tell tales of my throwing prowess until the end of time!"

"Stop showing off and let's eat," said Odin. "Light a fire, one of you."

"It's too hot out here in the sun," moaned Honir. "I'm not eating my lunch from my lap like a mortal peasant, either. I'm a god!"

"Perhaps we could shelter over there?" said Loki, pointing to a small stone house ahead of them. "We can pay them for our lodgings with the otter's pelt," he went on. "It's a particularly fine, glossy one after all."

"Fine. But let's disguise ourselves as mortals first," said Odin. "It won't do to have humans knowing our comings and goings."

"A disguise? You don't have to ask me twice," Loki replied, immediately changing his shining, handsome face into a more ordinary human one. The other gods followed suit, shifting their features into new, unremarkable faces.

When they reached the cottage, Odin rapped on the door. A tall, middle-aged man answered. He seemed confused when he saw them, as though he was expecting someone else.

"Yes?" he barked.

"Maybe we should go," Honir whispered to Odin. "I don't think he likes us."

But Loki wasn't put off. "Good day," he said, in his most charming voice. "We were wondering if we might shelter from the heat of the noonday sun in your beautiful home? We will give you a taste of this fine, fat fish in return," he said, holding up the salmon. "And I also present to you this otter. Its skin would make a beautiful hat, or perhaps a nice warm pair of gloves." Loki held up the otter for inspection, beaming with pride.

A dark expression passed over the man's face. He glared at them, each in turn. Then, after a pause, he snatched the salmon and the otter. "You had better come in," he snapped.

He showed them to a large dusty room with a couple of chairs and a bed and, without another word, slammed the door.

"How rude!" said Odin.

"Perhaps he's embarrassed because his house is so humble?" said Loki. "I know we're in disguise, but we're still very well-dressed. Especially me."

"Loki..." said Odin, with a note of warning in his voice. "What did I say about showing off?"

"I'll be quiet. In fact, I think I'll have a nap," said Loki. He yawned and curled up like a cat in his chair. "All this exploring is exhausting."

The three gods settled down to rest and soon drifted off into a doze.

When they woke, Loki blinked, trying to work out what was wrong. "I'm tied up!" he cried. Ropes bit cruelly into his chest, and his legs were bound to the chair.

"Me too!" cried Honir and Odin.

At that moment, three humans burst into the room, staring angrily down at them.

"I am Hreidmar the sorcerer," said the man who'd opened the door to them. "And these are my sons. Don't try to escape. The ropes are magical. They could bind any creature in the nine realms – even a god could not escape!"

"Why have you tied us up?" asked Loki, rather annoyed with himself. *Falling asleep in the house of a hostile stranger... not your most cunning move, Loki.*

"Let us go at once!" roared Odin.

Hreidmar gave Odin a look of pure, hot hatred. "Let you go? Never! That otter you killed was my son. Now you must pay for your terrible crime."

"Your *son*?" said Odin. He glared at Loki.

"Ah," said Loki. "This is awkward."

"Silence!" One of the younger men stepped forward. "He was our dear brother. I am Fafnir. This is Regin. I'm telling you so you know exactly who is going to end your miserable lives." His eyes glinted with violent fury.

"I don't understand," said Honir, still catching up. "How can your son be an otter?"

"Fool!" spat the sorceror. "He could change his

shape, of course. He was the son of a sorceror!" Hreidmar stifled an angry sob. "He used to spend every day fishing by the waterfall in his beautiful otter shape, bringing us back fish to eat. And now he's dead by your hand."

"And was the salmon a relative of yours too?" asked Loki.

The sorcerer just snarled in response.

"You're not making this better," Odin hissed.

"Father," said Regin, turning to the sorceror. "Let me slay these monsters. I will avenge our fallen brother!"

"No, *I* will," cried Fafnir, stepping forward. "I'm the eldest, it is my right!"

As the brothers squabbled, a plan assembled itself in Loki's mind. With his vast store of cunning, it only took a moment.

"We are very sorry for our terrible error," he began. "It was an honest mistake. But I should tell you, we are, in truth, gods in disguise."

With that, he changed back into his glowing, godly form. The other gods followed suit, their faces transforming so they shone like the sun.

Hreidmar looked slightly surprised, but then he laughed. "So?" he said. "You're still my prisoners. I'm the greatest sorceror in all the realms. I'm not afraid of the Aesir, or any other kind of god for that matter."

"Forgive me, mighty one," said Loki, changing tack, "but, as gods, we have great wealth and power. Perhaps we could give you a generous gift of gold, to show you how truly sorry we are?"

At the mention of gold, greedy fire glinted in the eyes of the three men.

Loki breathed a silent sigh of relief. *Mortals are so predictable*, he thought.

"We accept," said Hreidmar. "You must bring us the finest dwarf gold, and lots of it. Enough to cover the body of my murdered son."

"And enough to fill his skin, too," added Fafnir.

"And to cover every single whisker," chimed in Regin. "You – go!" he said to Loki, untying his bonds. "We'll keep the others as prisoners until you return."

Loki rubbed his wrists, relieved to be free, and rushed out of the cottage. He had no intention of handing over any of Asgard's beautiful gold, especially not any gold that belonged to him. But he knew exactly where to get the treasure he needed. He'd heard of a pool in Midgard, beneath a thundering waterfall, where a gigantic fish lived.

At least, it looked like a fish, but Loki knew it was a shape-shifting dwarf named Andvari, owner of a vast treasure hoard.

I'll need to catch him, thought Loki. *But who shall I ask to help me? Aha! The sea goddess, Ran. If anyone can catch a magical fish, it's her.* And he sped off towards the ocean.

"Oh splendid goddess," he called out when he reached the shore. "Will you grant lowly Loki an audience?"

The goddess rose up from the sea, glistening with foam and fury. "Why are you bothering me? I was down among the shipwrecks, counting treasure. You've made me lose my place."

"What a coincidence," said Loki. "It's treasure I want to talk to you about."

Ran looked suddenly interested. "Oh yes?"

Loki put on his most serious expression. "Yes. You see, the wicked dwarf Andvari has been boasting that his treasure hoard is greater and more precious than anything you've ever found in the sea," said Loki, "which of course is false."

Ran grew furious. "How dare he? The treasures I find when I wreck men's ships are magnificent. I will crush him for his insolence! I will…"

"No need, sweet goddess," said Loki. "I am happy to catch and punish him personally for spreading such lies. The snag is, I don't know how."

Without another word, Ran bobbed down beneath the waves, and came up clutching an enchanted net. "I use this to snare ships," she said. "But it will work just as well on a filthy lying dwarf!"

With that, she dived back into sea with an almighty splash and spray of salt. Loki ran straight for the waterfall, clutching the dripping net and whooping with delight.

The next part was easy. Loki simply flung the enchanted net into Andvari's waterfall and, seconds later, an enormous fish was flailing around in it, trapped in the magical mesh.

Loki gave a heave and pulled the creature out of the water. With a flash of sunlight on scales, the fish began to change shape. Fins stretched out to become arms; the tail divided into stumpy legs.

Soon, the being thrashing in the net was a furious dwarf. "Let me go!" Andvari yelled.

Loki grinned. "Now, Andvari, you can't escape

this magical net, however hard you try. But I promise to let you go if you pay me with gold from your treasure hoard."

"As you wish," grumbled Andvari. "I'll take you to my hoard if you let me out."

With a gloating smile, Loki released him and followed Andvari to his treasure, hidden in a cave behind the waterfall. The gorgeous, glinting pile of gold took Loki's breath away. He filled a bag with shining golden pieces; enough to cover the dead otter's body and to stuff it, too. Loki was about to leave when he spotted a beautiful ring on Andvari's finger. "I'll have that as well," he demanded, "for myself."

"Never!" said Andvari. "It's a magic ring and I use it to make more gold. If you take it, I'll be the poorest dwarf in all the realms."

"Tough," said Loki. Dangling the net over Andvari as a threat, he tugged the ring from the dwarf's finger. Then Loki ran off, with the bag of gold over one shoulder and the net over the other.

Andvari was hopping up and down in rage. "Then I curse my gold!" he yelled after Loki's departing back. "I curse my gold and that ring and anyone who owns it. And I hope you die a painful death too, Loki. Slow and agonizing!"

Loki's voice came back to him, faint on the wind. "I'm not afraid of curses. I'm the trickster and I make my own fate."

As soon as he reached Hreidmar's house, Loki proudly showed off his hoard of treasure.

"Cover the body of our dear brother and prove that you've brought enough gold," Regin grunted.

"Yes," said Fafnir, "And we've skinned him, so

you can stuff him with gold, too."

"How, um, thoughtful," Loki replied.

"Gold," murmured Hreidmar, gazing at the treasure like a man in love.

"Go on, Loki," said Odin. "Cover him and stuff the otterskin. Then you can come and undo these ropes. They're starting to pinch!"

Loki poured out the gold onto the floor. He filled the insides of the otterskin with it, then heaped the rest over the body and the fully-stuffed skin.

"I can still see one of his whiskers," Hreidmar complained, peering down at the glistening pile.

Loki looked at Andvari's ring on his finger. He'd been meaning to keep it. *Imagine the fun I could have with a cursed ring*, he thought. *But a deal's a deal.* With a sigh, he dropped the ring onto the pile, covering the otter's last whisker.

Hreidmar, Fafnir and Regin clustered around the gold, counting it, running it through their fingers, deaf and blind to everything but the sparkling magnificence of their treasure.

Loki was annoyed that their captors were enjoying themselves so much. "It's cursed, you know," he said, hoping to spoil their fun.

But the three men didn't hear, or didn't care.

Loki shrugged. "Can't say I didn't warn you."

"Will you free me and Odin?" asked Honir, looking pleadingly at Loki.

Loki strode over and untied their knots. "I'm sure you'll both agree," he said, "me saving the day quite outweighs any otter-related accidents?"

Odin grunted. "Come, let us return to Asgard. I am growing tired of this adventure. I believe a feast is in order."

"Good," said Loki. "I'm so hungry I could eat my own head!"

"Me too!" said Honir. "Although not *your* head, Loki. Knowing you, it would only play tricks on my stomach."

The three gods slipped away into the night. Hreidmar, Regin and Fafnir didn't even notice. They only had eyes for the gold.

Fafnir slipped the ring on his finger and watched it catch the light. "How beautiful it is," he murmured.

"Give me that!" cried Hreidmar. "I'm your father. This treasure belongs to me."

"We deserve a share too," protested Regin. "You can't have it all, Father!"

"That's right," said Fafnir, reaching for his sword. "And if you won't give it freely..." In the blink of an eye, his sword was up to its hilt in his father's chest. With a moan, Hreidmar fell onto the pile of treasure, scattering coins before him.

The curse had claimed its first victim.

Regin gasped with horror, but Fafnir began to laugh. "All mine, brother! It's all mine! Hahaha!" His laugh became a roar and as he roared, his body started to change. It swelled, becoming larger and scalier, while his face grew longer and wings sprouted out of his back. Soon, he was no longer a man, but a dragon.

"B...b...brother?" stammered Regin.

"Did you think our father was the only sorceror in the family? Or that our brother was the only one who could change his shape?"

Fafnir roared once more, breathing out a jet of flame that Regin only narrowly escaped. "No one will take my treasure from me now!" Fafnir declared. "And anyone who tries will be roasted like an ox on a spit." With that, he gathered up the treasure in his claws and launched into the air

on his mighty, leathery wings.

Fafnir the dragon flew far, far away, until he reached a cave large enough for his great dragon bulk. There, he settled down on top of the mound of gold, with one eye ever open for thieves. Especially thieves who answered to the name of Regin.

Sigurd the Dragonslayer

Sigurd had a destiny. He'd known it all his life: *One day I will slay the evil dragon, Fafnir.* Sigurd's real father had died many years ago and he'd been adopted by a blacksmith named Regin, who always treated him kindly.

"Fafnir killed my father," Regin had told him. "When you are old enough, you must kill this terrible monster."

Sigurd grew to be both strong and handsome, with golden hair, broad shoulders and eyes as blue as the sea. Regin made him train every day until he was a mighty warrior. He couldn't wait to prove he was the mightiest in the land.

After slaying a pack of wolves in the forest one day, he realized that he was finally ready to face Fafnir. "Just tell me where this dragon is, Regin, and I will kill him for you. I vow to avenge your father's death with dragon's blood."

Regin smiled. "First, you'll need a horse," he said. "You must go to the forest and catch yourself a steed. Fafnir's cave is far away."

"Of course," said Sigurd, and he set off in search of wild horses. But inside the forest he saw only one horse – and it didn't seem wild at all. It was standing calmly beside an old man, who was holding its bridle.

"Come here, boy," said the man.

"I'm no boy," Sigurd replied. He stood up straight and puffed out his chest. "I'm a warrior and soon I'll be a dragonslayer." But he found himself obeying the man and walking closer, all the same. He saw that the old man had only one eye... *Just like the great god, Odin*, he thought.

"Exactly like him," said the old man, as though reading his mind. "I *am* Odin." He raised his arms and a golden light began to shine around him. "Now," said the god. "I believe Loki has caused your stepfather some trouble?"

"I don't know what you mean," said Sigurd. "Regin never said anything about him."

Odin waved his hand. "It's a long story. But I'd like to give you this horse in payment for Loki's troublemaking."

Odin held out the horse's reins to Sigurd. "The horse is called Grani. He's as fast as the wind and will take you wherever you want to go."

"Thank you!" said Sigurd, taking the bridle.

Odin gave a solemn nod. "One more thing. To slay the dragon, you must use the sword your mother gave you before she died."

Sigurd felt bewildered. "That sword's broken," he began. But Odin had already vanished.

Sigurd leaped onto his magnificent new horse and galloped home to Regin.

"Look, Regin," he called as he rode up to their cottage. "The great god Odin gave me a horse!"

"Gods," growled Regin. "Can't trust them as

far as you can throw 'em." He looked the horse up and down with suspicion. "But the horse does look very fine and fast," he admitted.

"Odin also told me that I should use the sword my mother gave me, to slay the dragon," said Sigurd. "But it's in pieces," he added. "So I'm not sure what he meant by that."

"Why would you take a broken sword into battle?" said Regin. "I'll forge you a new one myself." He set to work immediately, melting some metal until it was red hot, then hammering it into shape. Finally, he plunged the sword in cold water, until he held a sharp, steaming blade in his hand.

Sigurd's eyes grew wide. "I can't wait to try it out!" He took the sword and swung it around his head with a mighty swoosh, then brought it down on Regin's anvil.

The blade shattered into a dozen pieces.

With a sigh, Regin began again. After many hot, hard hours bent over his anvil, he handed Sigurd an even stronger-looking sword.

"Thank you!" said Sigurd. Without a pause, he swung the sword and brought it down with all his strength on the anvil.

This time, the sword bit down into the anvil. But still it shattered with the force of Sigurd's blow.

Regin looked embarrassed. He brought out Sigurd's broken sword. "Perhaps I should make a new sword from these pieces?"

He set to work once more, heating the broken shards and hammering them together, feeling the metal take shape beneath his hands, almost of its own accord. Finally, he handed the glistening sword to Sigurd, who swung it around his head and brought it down with an almighty CLANG!

This time, the sword stayed in one piece. It was the anvil that split in two.

Sigurd was delighted. "Now just point the way and I'll slay that dragon!"

Regin handed him a map, the dragon's lair in a valley clearly marked upon it. Sigurd leaped onto his new horse, Grani, waving his newly-forged sword over his head. "Go, Grani!" he urged.

Grani seemed to fly along, hooves eating up the miles. Soon Sigurd reached the cave where Fafnir lay upon his golden hoard. The cave mouth was littered with small, white boulders.

Only as he rode closer did Sigurd realize they weren't boulders at all. They were human skulls.

Sigurd shuddered. *But I won't turn back*, he told himself. He already had a plan: Regin had told him that Fafnir stalked out from his cave each day to drink water from the river and catch animals to eat.

Sigurd climbed into a rocky crevice beside the river and waited...

After two leg-cramping hours, Fafnir emerged from his cave. The dragon was even larger than Sigurd had imagined, and covered in blood-red scales. Powerful muscles rippled beneath the scaly skin and his nostrils spewed out poisonous fumes. Sigurd covered his face as the dragon approached.

The creature dragged his long body over the crevice. Sigurd leaped out, stabbing his sword into the monster's soft underside. The blade punctured Fafnir's chest and plunged deep into the dragon's heart, letting out a jet of blood.

"Roaaaaaaargh!" Fafnir reared up on his hind legs with a bellow of pain. Sigurd stepped back, clutching his bloody sword.

"Puny human! How dare you prick me with your pathetic needle?" roared Fafnir. "It'll take more than that to kill the mighty Fafnir!"

He roared again, but much more weakly. The creature was dying.

Sigurd almost felt sorry for the beast as he clutched his bleeding chest and groaned in pain.

"Wicked thief," croaked the dragon. His voice was very faint now. Tiny puffs of smoke stuttered from his nostrils. "Did my brother send you to take away my treasure?"

"Who's your brother?" asked Sigurd.

The dragon let out an evil chuckle that turned into a cough. "Let me guess... Regin didn't tell you that I wasn't always a dragon? That I am his brother, and it was our father I slew?"

The dragon smiled at Sigurd's confusion. "Well, tell him from me that I hope he enjoys the deadly curse this treasure brings. I hope you enjoy it too, Dragonslayer. Soon, you'll perish... just like me," he whispered. He fell to the ground, coughed once more and died.

Sigurd looked down at Fafnir's body. "I don't fear this curse," he told himself. "All men die eventually. Why shouldn't I die rich?"

On top of the dragon's hoard he saw a beautiful golden ring. Sigurd slipped it on his finger, gathered the rest of the hoard in Grani's saddlebags and rode back to Regin. "I killed the dragon, Regin," he said. "But, why didn't you tell me that he was your brother?"

Regin shook his head sadly. "I didn't want to tell you of our family's shame. What my brother did was so terrible."

"I understand." Sigurd nodded, satisfied. "Now, let's share this gold and live like kings!"

"Wonderful," said Regin, with a dead-eyed smile. "But, can you do one last thing for me? Cut out the dragon's heart and cook it."

"Why?" asked Sigurd.

"I'll tell you when you return. Just make sure

you cook the heart thoroughly. Take your time."

Leaving the treasure with Regin, he rode to the dragon's cave and cut out Fafnir's heart. He roasted it over a fire, next to the dragon's body.

Now that the fire-breathing monster was dead, animals were returning to the valley. Birds flew overhead, filling the air with their songs.

As the meat cooked, it spat out fat and blood. A tiny drop landed on Sigurd's tongue. With the hot, salty taste in his mouth, he realized that the birdsong around him was forming into words.

"Drink a dragon's blood and you'll understand our speech," sang a passing crow.

"Listen carefully and it could save your life," cried an eagle overhead. "I spy danger, mortal man. Beware. Beware!"

Then a blackbird landed on a rock beside

his fire. "While you're busy cooking, Regin's sneaking up on you," it sang. "He knew he couldn't beat you in a fair fight.

But he'll kill you, Sigurd, so beware, beware."

"Now he has the treasure, he's coming for you," called the eagle. "Beware, beware!"

Sigurd froze. He heard crunching footsteps behind him. Grabbing his sword, he was on his feet in seconds. Just as the birds had warned, Regin was running straight at him, his own sword drawn, his face filled with fury.

But Sigurd was too quick for the older man. He plunged Gram into Regin's chest.

Regin grunted and crumpled to his knees. He looked up at Sigurd, his eyes burning with hate.

"The treasure's yours now," he growled.

"And so's the curse." Then he fell forward, beside his dragon brother Fafnir.

"Oh Regin!" cried Sigurd. "You were like a father to me. How could you betray me like this?" He stayed a while, weeping. Then, with one last look at the bodies, Sigurd mounted his horse and headed towards Regin's home.

As he rode, the birds sang to him once more. "Ride on from here and don't turn left or right. Soon you'll come to a beautiful maiden asleep inside a ring of fire. Her name is Brynhild and she will need your help."

Sigurd nodded his thanks. Although his heart was full of grief, he couldn't let that stop him.

I'm a hero, he told himself. *I've slain the dragon. Now it's time to save the beautiful Brynhild.*
And he rode on, towards a new adventure.

Brynhild and the Ring of Fire

A tall young woman strode into Odin's throne room and bowed low before the father of the gods. "You called for me, my lord?" she said.

Odin nodded and rose from his throne. "Welcome, Brynhild. Walk with me and I will show you the next mortal I want you to save. He's in the thick of a bloody battle as we speak. Quickly, it is almost time."

Brynhild's eyes lit up at the mention of battle. She followed Odin to the walls of Asgard with swift, eager steps, her chain mail clinking as she walked, her sword gripped in her hand.

Brynhild was one of the Valkyries – a race of supernatural warrior women. As a Valkyrie, it was her duty to rescue the bravest mortal fighters at the moment of death, and to carry them up to Valhalla, the golden hall of the gods, to enjoy an afterlife of fights and lavish feasts.

Odin pointed to a battle raging far below. "Your task is to bring me the mighty old king with the long beard. He's the man I want. See how fiercely he fights. Go!"

Brynhild summoned her enchanted chariot with

a whistle and flew downwards with a whoop of joy. As the battle roar rose around her, she slowed her chariot and scanned the scene. Among all the men fighting for their lives, she spotted the king that Odin wanted her to rescue.

Brynhild hovered for a while, invisible to the men below her, watching the old warrior fight. The king was strong and brave, certainly, but the man he fought was stronger and braver still.

With a flash of speed, she rode her chariot into the thick of the battle and grabbed the king's opponent. Then she swung him on board and took him with her, up to the hall of the gods.

Surely Odin will he even more pleased with this fine man? she thought.

When Brynhild saw the Allfather's face, she realized that she couldn't have been more wrong.

"How dare you?" roared Odin. "I gave you my orders. This is the wrong man!"

Brynhild opened her mouth to argue, but Odin hurled her over the walls of Asgard, sending her plummeting down towards Midgard below.

"Any Valkyrie who disobeys me is a Valkyrie no longer," Odin bellowed after her.

She fell down... and down... and down...

"As your punishment, you will sleep in an enchanted hall, surrounded by a ring of fire. You'll only awake when a man is brave enough to pass through the flames and take you as his wife. And when you wake, you will be a mortal woman. You've disgraced the noble name of the Valkyries!"

With Odin's words ringing in her ears, Brynhild smacked down onto a cold stone slab. All around her, she heard the crackling of flames.

Her eyes fluttered closed and she drifted into a deep sleep. The last words she heard were Odin's. "No one disobeys me. NO ONE!"

She seemed to sleep forever, dreaming of fire and battle and of falling but never landing, until at last, through the darkness, there came a voice.

She opened her eyes to see a man with golden hair, broad shoulders and sea-blue eyes standing over her. The man was staring at her, enraptured. "My name is Sigurd," he said. "I've come to rescue you."

Brynhild shook the grogginess from her mind, trying to remember where she was and what had happened. "I was falling…" she murmured. But as her head cleared, she grasped her rescuer's hand and sat up. "My name's Brynhild. Are you really here to free me?"

Sigurd helped her to her feet. "I am, my lady," he said. "My steed is strong, he can carry us both through the flames." Then Brynhild remembered Odin's last words to her. "I can't leave. The king of the gods has trapped me here. I can only escape if a man is willing to marry me. But I don't know how to be a wife. All my life, I've been a warrior."

Sigurd clasped her hands in his. "As am I! I would love to marry you, brave Brynhild. Please, take this ring as a pledge of my love."

Brynhild smiled as the handsome young warrior slipped a golden ring onto her finger. She'd seen many fighting men in her time, but none had ever been quite so beautiful or gentle. His voice was soft and sad, as though he had been through terrible hardships.

"This ring is just one portion of my fortune," said Sigurd. "Let me ride to the place where my treasure lies, so I can buy us a home and pay for the wedding. Then I will return for you." With a smile and a bow, he left.

Brynhild stared after him, longingly.

Sigurd rode away, bursting with happiness and hope. He waved at the birds in the sky above him. "Thank you, kind birds! You saved me from Regin, and then you led me to the most beautiful woman I've ever seen. A woman who knows how to fight with a sword, too! I don't think life could get any better."

The birds called back. Their voices were urgent,

as though they wanted to warn him of something, but the dragon's blood was wearing off. Sigurd could only hear trills and cheeps. He shrugged off a creeping feeling of unease and galloped towards Regin's home, his heart full of eager love. He couldn't wait to take the treasure to his beautiful Brynhild.

It was starting to get dark now, and Sigurd turned this way and that through gloomy woods until he was no longer sure where he was going. When he finally saw a majestic hall ahead, he spurred his horse on. *I can ask for directions back to Regin's village*, he thought.

At the hall, Sigurd was welcomed by servants and taken to see the king and queen.

"Welcome," said the queen. "We have heard that a brave warrior has killed the dragon who was terrifying our people. Could that warrior be you?" She smiled. "You must be very rich, now that the dragon's gold is yours."

Sigurd looked awkward and shuffled his feet. "I suppose I am," he said.

"You are welcome here!" cried the queen. "Gudrun, take this hero to his seat." She gestured to a beautiful princess, who smiled at Sigurd and led him to a cushioned bench, then plied him with food and drink. He had never eaten such a delicious meal nor drunk such fine mead.

All the while, the princess made sure his glass was full, listening patiently while he raved about Brynhild, a woman he was going to rescue from a ring of fire.

Princess Gudrun smiled as she poured the mead. So did her mother the queen, who knew something Gudrun didn't. *Oh Sigurd, you won't be rescuing Brynhild tomorrow*, she thought. *This drink has a secret ingredient that will make you forget all about her. Then, dear Sigurd, your handsome face and your hoard of dragon's treasure will belong to my darling Gudrun.*

In the morning, Sigurd awoke with the feeling that there was somewhere he should be, but he couldn't think where.

"I have an idea!" exclaimed the queen, as Sigurd approached the breakfast table with a faraway look in his eyes. "You and my daughter should be married. Seeing you together last night, I know you'll make a wonderful couple."

"What do you think, Sigurd?" said Gudrun, in a shy voice. "Shall we be married?"

"Well, I do think I'm in love," said Sigurd. He felt as though he were deep under warm water, looking up at blurry lights. "I... I will marry you."

"Now go and fetch your treasure so you can buy a beautiful new home for my darling daughter," said the queen.

So Sigurd rode off to fetch his treasure hoard from Regin's house. He stuffed the gold into his saddlebags, along with a few old books of magic that belonged to Regin's father.

Then he settled down to a quiet life with his new wife Gudrun in a fine hall by the sea. From time to time, he felt a wave of sadness that he couldn't explain. On those low days, he distracted himself by learning spells from Regin's books.

Years passed, until Gudrun's younger brother, Gunnar, came of age and wanted to find himself a wife. He asked his sister and his brother-in-law, Sigurd, if they knew of any suitable woman.

An image came swimming up from the depths of Sigurd's memory. "I've heard there's a beautiful woman trapped in a ring of fire," he said. He frowned. "I'm not quite sure where she is. But I do remember that the man who's brave enough to jump into the ring of fire is the man who will set her free and marry her."

Gudrun felt a surge of anxiety. The night she met her husband, he had been raving about Brynhild. *Did he intend to marry her as well as rescue her back then?* The secret her mother had told her on her wedding night came rushing back. *Only my mother's enchanted mead stopped Sigurd from rescuing*

Brynhild. *What if Brynhild steals my husband away?* And then she thought, *But if she's already safely married to my brother, she wouldn't dare....*

"Yes, Gunnar," she said to her brother. "Of course you must marry her! You're the bravest man in the kingdom – after my handsome Sigurd. You're just the person to rescue her. I'm sure that Mother and Father would love to have you both to live with them." She didn't add... *far away from Sigurd and me.*

"Then it's settled," said Sigurd. "I'll come with you, brother-in-law. We will find her together!"

"Excellent!" said Gunnar. "Let's go at once."

The two men rode for days and nights, barely stopping, until they came to a high-walled hall surrounded by fire. Sigurd felt a flicker of a long-lost memory. "This place seems so familiar..." he murmured. "But I don't know why."

"Now to claim my bride!" cried Gunnar. He spurred his horse and made for the fire. But his horse refused to jump into the flames. It whinnied and stamped and would not budge.

"May I borrow your horse, Grani?" asked Gunnar. "Perhaps he's braver than this cowardly old nag."

"Of course," said Sigurd, hopping nimbly down from the saddle and holding out the reins to Gunnar.

As soon as Gunnar climbed onto Grani's back, the horse began to stamp its hooves and snort out puffs of air. Gunnar spurred the horse, but it bucked so hard, he was thrown to the ground with a heavy thump.

"I don't think your horse wants to go into the fire either," said Gunnar, stumbling to his feet.

"Perhaps if I ride him, he will?" said Sigurd. He felt a little offended on his horse's behalf and patted the creature's head. "Grani's never scared. But I think he only trusts me, don't you boy?"

"Well, there's no point *you* riding in and rescuing the girl to be your bride," said Gunnar. "You're already married to my sister!"

Sigurd shook his head. "I won't go to her as myself. Just watch," he said. Using a spell that he'd taught himself from one of Regin's old books of sorcery, he changed his shape so he looked exactly like Gunnar.

His brother-in-law stared, open-mouthed, as Sigurd leaped onto his horse crying, "Wait for me in the woods. I'll bring you back a bride!"

Sigurd rode bravely through the flames, just as he had done years ago – only this time, he wore Gunnar's face.

Past the fire and inside the walls, Sigurd saw a beautiful woman of about his own age. Something about her made his heart ache. She was so sad and yet so strong.

She looked him up and down. She seemed surprised to see him, but not particularly pleased. "Who are you?" she asked.

"I'm... Gunnar," he said, staring at the beautiful woman. "I'm here to rescue you. Will you marry me?" he asked, although in that moment, he wished he was asking for himself.

A look of pain crossed her beautiful face. "A man came years ago and promised he'd return for me. But that was long ago. So yes, I'll marry you, if you take me away from this awful place."

Sigurd smiled weakly and took Brynhild by the hand. They galloped on Grani through the flames. When they reached the woods, Sigurd asked Brynhild to wait for him, and rode into the trees where Gunnar was hiding behind a thicket of trees. "She's all yours," whispered Sigurd.

Gunnar clapped him on the back and went out to see his bride-to-be with his own eyes.

"Didn't you have a different horse a moment ago?" asked Brynhild, as Gunnar came out of the trees. "Its mane looked darker before."

Gunnar mumbled something about it being a magical horse that could change its appearance, and they trotted on in silence.

Gunnar carried his new bride off to his parents' royal hall and Sigurd went back to his own wife, and his home by the sea. But he often dreamed of a fierce female warrior clad all in chain mail and armed with a sword.

Brynhild, meanwhile, was far from happy. *I wish I'd never fallen to this mortal realm. I wish I could go back to being a Valkyrie.* But she also wished that she could see Sigurd once more.

When her sister-in-law, Gudrun, arrived to visit one day, she welcomed the distraction. They went for a walk beside the river. They were chatting about their husbands, boasting about their courage. Brynhild felt it was the sort of thing expected of a fine lady, though she would much rather have been boasting of her own battle skills.

"My husband's so brave, he rode through a ring of fire to rescue me," she said.

Gudrun shook her head, annoyed on Sigurd's behalf. "That's not true! It was *my* husband who rescued you," she said. She instantly regretted it, but she couldn't take it back now.

Brynhild frowned. "But I haven't even met your husband. I don't understand."

Gudrun gulped. "You have met him, Brynhild. His name is Sigurd. He did a spell to make himself look like my brother. I forget why. Something about my brother's cowardly horse... "

Brynhild suddenly felt ice-cold. *Sigurd. The man who abandoned me. How could he?* "Your husband is... Sigurd?"

"Yes," said Gudrun. She tensed to see how Brynhild would react. Brynhild said nothing, so she went on, with a story that was not *quite* the truth. The dangerous scowl on Brynhild's face made her quite sure that the truth would not end well for her. "He came to my parents' hall one day and he fell in love with me at first sight. Well, more or less," she said.

Rage rose in Brynhild's heart, but not at Gudrun. *He betrayed me.* "I have to go," she said, and ran back along the river path.

Gudrun watched her go, hoping that Brynhild would not rush to Sigurd and declare her love.

That night, Brynhild turned to her husband. "I know the truth about the day we met," she said in a quiet, furious voice. "You deceived me. To make amends, you can do one thing. Kill Sigurd... or I'll kill him myself."

Gunnar was stunned. "I can see why you might

be angry with me for the trick I played to win you, but why do you want *him* dead?"

"Because he promised to marry me and he broke his promise," snarled Brynhild. Her teeth were clenched, and some of her Valkyrie spirit flashed in her eyes.

Feeling a fury of his own at the idea of his wife pining after another man, Gunnar *wanted* to kill Sigurd. "But he is married to my sister. I can't."

"Fine," snarled Brynhild. So she sent a servant to the room where Sigurd slept beside Gudrun. Under her instructions, the man took Sigurd's own sword and stabbed him through the heart.

"My husband, my husband!" Gudrun cried, waking to find Sigurd dying beside her. She ran outside, screaming for help.

A few moments later, another figure entered

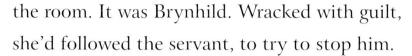

the room. It was Brynhild. Wracked with guilt, she'd followed the servant, to try to stop him.

"Too late," she murmured, taking Sigurd's hand. "Oh my love, I was so angry. Forgive me."

Sigurd did not reply. He was already dead.

Brynhild took the bloody sword that had killed Sigurd and thrust it without a moment's hesitation into her own heart.

It seemed only a moment later that Brynhild was aware of the sun on her face and a soft, sweet breeze. The air smelled like honey and roses, with the faint, sharp tang of the sea.

Brynhild looked about her and saw green grass and flowers and, a little way off, a golden hall with its doors wide open. A very familiar hall.

"It's Valhalla!" she cried. "I never thought I'd see this place again."

"Brynhild?" came a voice. It was Sigurd.

"You're here too," she cried. Her expression hardened for a moment. "Why did you leave me in the ring of fire?" she asked.

Sigurd shook his head. "I can't be sure, but I think I was under a spell," he said. He held out his hands to her. "It doesn't matter now."

Brynhild hung her head. "But Sigurd... how can you ever forgive me?
I had you killed."

Sigurd smiled at her. "Fate's played some cruel tricks on us. But, finally, we can be together."

Brynhild let out a cry of joy as Sigurd put his arms around her. "Thank the gods!" she said.

"I accept your thanks," said a voice from close behind them. It was Odin. "Welcome home, Valkyrie," he said. "Although you disobeyed me, you deserve to be repaid for all the pain that Loki caused you with that wretched curse he set in motion. And you, too, Dragonslayer. Welcome."

Awestruck, Sigurd turned to Brynhild. "You were a Valkyrie?" he asked.

"I was," said Brynhild. She looked at Odin. "And I am ready to serve again, if you want me?"

Odin shook his head. "Not yet. But I may need both of you to fight for me one day."

"Then we will keep our swords sharp," said

Brynhild. The sound of battle cries came drifting towards them. "Shall we go and join the fray?"

Sigurd nodded, eyes shining with joy. He put his hand in hers, and they went to fight and feast with all the other brave warriors of Asgard.

"Excellent," said Loki, walking to Odin's side with Honir, as the couple walked away. "A happy ending, thanks to me."

Odin shot him an angry look. "Thanks to *you*? What do you mean? You started this whole mess by killing that otter and getting us captured!"

"And freeing us with cursed gold," said Honir.

Loki raised a finger. "No, no, no, you've got this all wrong." He gestured in the direction of Brynhild and Sigurd. "If I'd never killed that otter and then captured that dwarf and caused the curse, why, those two would never have met!"

"You're impossible!" snorted Odin. He pointed down to Midgard. "You do realize that Princess Gudrun has now inherited the treasure and is going to come to a sticky end *very* soon. That's hardly a happy ending, is it?"

"It's not as though she was entirely innocent," said Loki. "And her mother was wonderfully villainous, don't you think?"

"That still doesn't make *you* the hero of this story," scowled Odin.

"Perhaps," said Loki, with a twinkling smile. "But wouldn't life be dull without me?" With that, he strode off, whistling happily.

I hope Loki never arranges a happy ending for me, thought Odin, and he shuddered despite the warmth of the Asgardian day.

THE END OF THE WORLD

Nothing lasts forever, not even Asgard. With his gift of prophecy, Odin lived most of his life with the terrible knowledge that *Ragnarok* – the destruction of the gods – was coming. This is the story of the beginning of the end and Odin's vision of a world torn apart by battle, flames and hate.

Balder the Invincible

O f all the gods in Asgard, Balder was the most beautiful. But unlike many of them, he had a sweet and gentle nature. His mother, Frigg, and father, Odin, doted on him. In fact, all the gods loved him deeply – except for Loki. He thought Balder was a big, dull fool who was, irritatingly, more handsome than Loki himself.

So when Balder began to have terrible nightmares that he was going to die, almost all the gods (with one notable exception) were sick with worry.

Odin, who could see into the future, knew that these definitely weren't just dreams. "We must save our son," he declared.

Frigg nodded. "I'll make everything swear an oath not to hurt my darling Balder."

The goddess went out into the world and spoke to all the rocks and metals of Midgard, asking them to swear her oath. She gathered the promises of everything in nature, from poisonous plants and invisible diseases to ravenous bears and scorching fires.

On her way back to Asgard, she went to an oak tree, which pledged its oath to Balder. As she walked away, she noticed a little sprig of mistletoe, nestling in the oak's high branches. *But it's so small, it doesn't even have its own roots in the ground. I don't need to take an oath from that*, she thought to herself. She rushed back to the other gods. "Nature has promised never to hurt Balder," she said. "But how can we be sure it will keep its word and keep him safe?"

"Why don't we try a practical test?" suggested Loki, and lobbed a rock at Balder's head.

It bounced off without hurting him at all.

"Amazing!" said Balder, looking down at himself in disbelief.

All the gods laughed with relief. Since Loki's rock had done no harm, they started throwing larger, more dangerous objects at Balder.

"How about this?" cried one, throwing a sword. It bounced off Balder's chest.

"Or this?" cried another, hurling a spear with a cruelly sharp tip. That bounced off too.

Balder just laughed as each god in turn threw something heavy, sharp, hot or otherwise deadly at him.

Loki quickly grew bored. "What's the point in a game where no one loses?" he grumbled. The longer the gods went on with their harmless sport, the angrier he got, until he knew he had to put a stop to it.

The trickster turned himself into an old woman and went to find Frigg. "Do you know that some crowd of thugs are trying to stone a god to death back there?" the old woman asked.

Frigg smiled. "Oh, they're just playing a game. My son Balder is invincible, you see. I made everything in nature swear not to hurt him."

"Everything?" the woman croaked. "Even disgusting, deadly diseases?"

"Of course," said Frigg. "Especially diseases."

"Even rocks? Even mud? Even... cabbage?"

Frigg sighed. She was starting to wish she

hadn't been so polite to this old busybody. "Yes, everything." Then she remembered. "Except mistletoe. But that's hardly even a proper plant." Frigg looked up. The old woman had gone.

Loki, looking like himself once more, quickly found a sprig of mistletoe in Midgard. He plucked it and whittled the end of its stem into a point. Then he rushed back to the game.

At the edge of the cheering, laughing crowd stood Balder's blind brother, Hod. Loki sidled up to him and pinched him nastily.

"Hello Loki," sighed Hod.

"Why aren't you joining in?" asked Loki. "He's your brother, you should get to play!"

"I don't have any weapons, and even if I did, I can't see, so I can't aim them at him," said Hod.

"Nonsense. Here, take this twig. I'll help you

aim. You should do homage to your brother's amazing powers like everyone else!"

So Loki took Hod's hand, gave him the sharpened mistletoe twig, and put him in the right position to throw.

Hod released the twig. It sailed through the air and pierced Balder's heart. The beautiful, beloved god fell dead. All the gods fell silent...

...and Loki ran like a hunted deer, while everyone stood frozen, too shocked to stop him.

Then the gods began to weep and wail at their loss. Frigg threw herself on the ground, kissing Balder's cooling cheek and covering him in dripping tears. Balder's wife, Nanna, fell down beside his body and lay still. Her grief was so powerful, it had stopped her heart.

Hod was put in chains, but everyone knew

that Loki was really behind the crime.

"We must find him and punish him!" roared Odin. "I bet he's gone to Midgard."

"Not yet," wept Frigg. "Please, will someone go down to Helheim, where Balder's soul has fled, and beg Hel to let my Balder come back to me?"

"I shall go!" said Odin.

"No, Father," said a tall young god, named Hermod. "Hel hates you for banishing her. Let me go. She doesn't know me."

So Odin allowed Hermod to borrow Sleipnir, his eight-legged horse, and the young god rode into the depths of Helheim. He leaped over the walls of Hel's hall on the beast and rushed inside.

Hel looked up painfully slowly, fixing her half-rotten gaze on Hermod. "What... do... you... want?" Each word seemed heavy on her tongue.

"Please will you let my
brother Balder
come back to us?"
Hermod asked. "We
love him so much."

Hel sneered. "Love?
If he is... so... beloved, let...
everything... in creation... weep... for him. Then
I'll... let... him... go."

Hermod spurred Sleipnir on and rode all around
the world asking everyone to weep for Balder. He
asked men and women on Midgard, and they wept.
He asked the dwarves beneath the earth, and they
wept. He asked the giants in Jotunheim, and they
too wept for sweet, beautiful Balder.

But then Hermod came to an old giantess in a
cave. When he asked her to weep, she said, "Why

should I? He's nothing to me. I don't care at all."

Hermod rode away, not noticing the giantess behind him change back into a smirking Loki.

So poor Balder remained with Hel in Helheim, and the gods prepared his funeral pyre – or they tried to. Their shock and sadness had left them so distraught that they could barely lift Balder's body, so they called upon a giantess. The giantess rode into Asgard on a giant wolf, using poisonous snakes for reins. With her powerful arms bulging, she lowered Balder's body into a beautiful boat and pulled the vessel into the middle of a lake. There, she set it alight and the gods raised their voices in sobbing wails of grief.

As the flames licked at Balder's corpse, their thoughts soon turned to vengeance. Odin led the charge down to Midgard, with Tyr and Thor and

many mighty gods riding beside him.

When they caught up with Loki, he turned himself into a salmon and leaped into the river. But Thor grabbed hold and squeezed him, hard. "You've played your last trick," Thor snarled.

Even Loki knew he was beaten, and he prepared for death. But the gods had something worse in store. They took two of Loki's children and ripped out their entrails. Then they dragged him to a cave beneath Midgard and bound him with the guts. Odin hung a snake above Loki and its burning venom dripped onto his face. From time to time, his pain grew so great that his shudders caused earthquakes on Midgard above.

"Curse you, gods," howled Loki. "One day, I'll get my revenge."

But he would have to wait for a very long time.

Ragnarok

The years rolled by, marching faster and faster, like an eager army – or so it seemed to Odin. The world grew older although not more wise. Odin's single eye stared into the future and saw only destruction.

He had a vision of himself with Thor beside him. "Ragnarok is coming," he said. "The doom of the gods."

"Then we will die fighting!" Thor replied, with a shake of his hammer.

Odin surrendered himself to his vision and stepped into the future in his mind's eye. "But how do you fight the end of the world?" he asked.

Thor had no answer to that. They looked down at Midgard and saw chaos. Wars were breaking out in every land. A cruel, unending winter, known as the Fimbulwinter, swallowed every land.

Then the great wolves, who chased the chariots of the Sun and Moon, began to catch up with their prey. Earthquakes shook Midgard, raining rocks down onto the dwarves in their realm below.

A violent quake shook Midgard to its core and a shout rang out. "I'm free!" screamed Loki. "Free!"

The roof of his prison-cave was cracked and his bonds had been shaken loose. He climbed up into Midgard and gazed around at the destruction and the slaughter. "This is beautiful!" he laughed.

He knew now was the moment to take revenge for his imprisonment. "Come to me, my children!" he called. "Come to me, giants! Come, demons!

Let's finish those arrogant Aesir once and for all!"

Far away, Loki's son Fenrir burst free of his bonds. "I come, Father!" the wolf howled.

Hel herself slowly rose up from Helheim. "Coming... Father," Hel gasped.

A mighty fire demon named Surt left the inferno of Muspelheim for the first time, at the head of an army of demons. The world began to burn.

In the ocean, Jormungand the world serpent stirred. As he thrashed, the oceans rose and flooded Midgard, fighting with Surt's flames to see which could wreak the most havoc and destruction.

Loki and his army swarmed over Asgard's bridge, howling for blood. Lumbering giants of rock and ice brought all their pent-up rage against the gods. "Thor has killed so many of us," they roared. "We will crush those cruel Aesir beneath our feet!"

Heimdall, Asgard's guardian, heard the monsters long before they reached the bridge. His horn rang out and the gods prepared for war.

Odin summoned all the dead warriors and Valkyries in Asgard. "It's time to fight our final battle," he cried. "It's your duty to protect your gods! It's your chance to destroy our enemies!"

Brave Sigurd and mighty Brynhild put on their helmets. "To the death!" they cried. They knew it would be a final death this time.

Odin's forces gathered on a vast plain to wait...

Loki's army was thundering closer. Loki burst through the gates of Asgard, with his monstrous troops baying for Aesir blood close behind.

Jormungand slithered up onto the rainbow bridge, and it trembled beneath his terrible weight. As the last of Loki's warriors rode through Asgard's gates, the bridge cracked and crumbled. There was no way out.

The battle raged for many days, a clashing, snarling, blood-soaked nightmare of swords and teeth and claws and crushing clubs.

The wild wolf Fenrir swallowed Odin whole. "That's for keeping me prisoner," he growled.

Thor raised his hammer and hurled it at Jormungand. "Finally, snake, you're going to die!"

As the hammer hit home, the serpent spat a gob of poison. "I've beaten you!" said Thor. But his voice grew weak and he staggered to the ground. The poison flowed through his veins and death called him into darkness.

Heimdall and Loki stood face to face. Loki's eyes glowed with delight, while despair and fury burned in Heimdall's heart. "This is all your fault!" Heimdall cried. He brought his sharp blade down. Loki never laughed again.

Then Surt's flames licked up, engulfing everything, and Asgard was no more.

A New Beginning

Silence fell in Odin's vision. The world tree Yggdrasil was blackened by flames and drowned beneath Midgard's rising oceans. It seemed that nothing and no one had survived.

But then, on the horizon, a new sun rose, the child of the old sun. A fresh, young land drew itself out of the sea and the scorched world tree began to bloom once more.

A little crack opened in the tree, growing wider and wider, until it let out two humans, a man and a woman. Their names were Lif and Lifthrasir. The world tree had sheltered them, so that the human race would not be entirely destroyed.

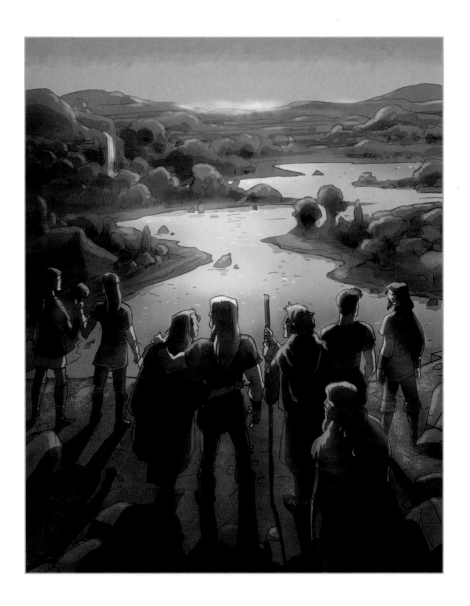

Out of the rubble of Asgard, a few lonely figures staggered into the sunlight, tattered and bloody but alive. Vidar and Vali, two sons of Odin, had survived the battle. Modi and Magni, the sons of Thor, emerged next, clutching Thor's hammer, Mjollnir, between them. They wept for their father, but they knew it was their duty to protect the world now that he was gone.

From beyond the shores of death came Balder and his wife, Nanna, his brother Hod, and Honir too. But no one else returned.

Balder looked out at the sparkling world. "We'll mourn our dead," he said. "But then we will start the race of gods again." His beautiful face smiled sadly. "And this time, I hope, we'll live in peace."

As the vision faded, Odin smiled. "Yes, my son. I hope so too."

Chart of the Nine Realms

YGGDRASIL
The world tree

ASGARD
Realm of the Aesir gods

The well
of Urd

Jormungand, the
world serpent

Bifrost, the rainbow bridge

JOTUNHEIM
Realm of giants

Ratatosk,
the squirrel

Yggdrasil's spreading branches cover every realm, from lofty Asgard to fiery Muspelheim.

Mimir's well

NIFELHEIM
Realm of ice

Nidhogg, the dragon

The Great Eagle

VANAHEIM
Realm of the Vanir gods

ALFHEIM
Realm of elves

MIDGARD
Realm of people

NIDAVELLIR
Realm of dwarves

HELHEIM
Realm of the dead

MUSPELHEIM
Realm of fire

Surt, the fire demon

Where the Norse Myths came from

Until the arrival of Christianity, around a thousand years ago, Norsemen across Scandinavia worshipped the gods of their ancestors. Poets learned stories about the gods by heart. Over time, the names of some gods and parts of the stories changed, and sometimes new twists crept in.

Odin was always the king of the gods, and was worshipped by chieftains and noblemen. Thor was the god of ordinary people, while warriors followed Tyr, god of combat. Women paid special reverence to Frigg, goddess of marriage and motherhood.

Even though no one worships the Norse gods

today, their names live on in the days of the week. 'Tuesday' comes from *Tiw*, the Old English form of Tyr. 'Wednesday' comes from *Woden*, Old English for Odin. 'Thursday' is Thor's day, and 'Friday' is Frigg's day.

The very oldest written accounts of the Norse myths date back to the 9th century, from a collection of songs known as the *Poetic Edda*. Then, in the 13th century, Icelandic poet Snorri Sturluson put together a collection of tales of the gods known as the *Prose Edda*.

Another unknown author wrote down a story called the *Volsunga Saga*, which tells the epic tale of Sigurd and Brynhild. This saga, along with the Eddas, inspired two legendary works: J.R.R. Tolkein's tales of Middle Earth, and composer Richard Wagner's *Ring Cycle* operas.

Usborne Quicklinks

For links to websites where you can find out more about the people and places mentioned in the Norse myths, examine objects from the age of the Vikings and find a pronunciation guide to the names of Norse gods, go to the Usborne Quicklinks Website at **www.usborne.com/ quicklinks** and enter the keywords: **norse myths**.

When using the internet, please follow the internet safety guidelines shown on the Usborne Quicklinks website. The links at Usborne Quicklinks are regularly reviewed and updated, but Usborne Publishing is not responsible and does not accept liability for the content on any website other than its own. We recommend that all children are supervised while using the internet.

Edited by Susanna Davidson and Lesley Sims

Designed by Caroline Spatz

Expert advice from Dr. Anne Millard
With thanks to Katrina Johnson

Additional design by Samantha Barrett

Digital manipulation by Nick Wakeford and John Russell

First published in 2013 by Usborne Publishing Ltd., Usborne House, 83-85 Saffron Hill, London EC1N 8RT, England. www.usborne.com
Copyright © 2013 Usborne Publishing Ltd.